Never Fool a Duke
Willful Wallflowers Book Two

Claudia Stone

This book is dedicated to Iris Lloyd, a reader.

CONTENTS

ACKNOWLEDGMENTS

As ever, I am extremely grateful to my copyeditor Emma Hamilton for her support throughout the writing process. Thanks go as well to all the readers who patiently waited for Book Two. Apologies that it took so long – this book is my "pandemic baby".

And finally, to Conal, my own duke in shining armor (or farmer in muddy wellies!). Thank you for your love, support, patience, our three strapping boys, and for being my muse. One day I'll get you to pose for a cover picture!

PROLOGUE

There are two sides to every story. Two sides to a coin. There are even, when one thinks on it, two sides to midnight.

Mr Waldo Havisham had never given this last fact any contemplation until the moment that his daughter decided to make her debut into the world. He had just poured himself a large measure of brandy and was about to light a cheroot so that he might celebrate—in a most masculine manner—the birth of his first child, when a knock came upon the door.

"Mr Havisham, it is your wife," the chambermaid whispered nervously, as Waldo answered her knock.

For a moment, Waldo stilled, as he experienced the peculiar sensation of time itself halting. Childbirth was a dangerous thing, and while moments ago, he might have been celebrating his son's birth, there was every possibility that he might now be confronted with his wife's death.

"What about my wife?" he queried, resisting the urge to take the chambermaid by the shoulders and shake her until she answered. Good staff were hard to find, and even more so when one was entrenched in the wilds of the Outer Hebrides.

"The accoucheur," the maid replied, her tongue tripping slightly on the unfamiliar word, "believes that Mrs Havisham is still labouring."

"And what on earth does that mean?" Waldo, who was near apoplectic with worry, did not have the mental capacity to try and decipher the young woman's announcement.

"It means twins, Mr Havisham."

Twins? Waldo had not contemplated that his virility might be so great that he could sire two children in one night, but it must be so if a second child was on the way.

Feeling rather pleased with himself, Waldo bid the maid to take her leave, but as she turned on her heel, the clocks of the house began to strike the hour,

1

their chimes ringing merrily through the halls.

"Gracious," Waldo paused, "It's midnight."

"Haud Hogmanay," the maid whispered.

"Ne' rday," Waldo replied, without missing a beat.

The last day of December had brought Waldo a son, and soon he would learn that the first day of the New Year had brought him a daughter. For twins to be born on separate days was rare, though not unheard of, but for a pair to be born a year apart was nothing short of unusual. Which worried Waldo, for he had spent a lifetime battling the unusual circumstances into which he had been born.

Waldo was the heir apparent to a Barony by writ, which, thanks to its antiquity, was eligible to pass through the female line, unlike newer titles which were created by patent and could only be inherited by male progeny.

The current holder of the Baronetcy of Hebrides was Waldo's Aunt Phoebe, a woman so eccentric that Waldo often wondered if it might not have been better for the title to have fallen into abeyance, rather than fall into her hands. Lady Havisham had spent years frittering away the estate's meagre income on exploring the world. Then, to add insult to the injury of her ancestral line, when she had returned from her travels, she had invited artists, bohemians, and bluestockings to take up residence in Hebrides Hall, which was located on the largest of the archipelago's isles, Lewis and Harris. During the summer months, when the season finished, Hebrides Hall was a veritable den of iniquity, as bohemians and egalitarians summered there, at Aunt Phoebe's invitation.

Waldo's mother, a paragon of grace, virtue, and sensibility, had oft despaired to her young son about the eccentricities of his aunt. Thus, when she and his father—a barrister by trade—had died after a nasty carriage accident on the road to Fort Augustus, and Waldo had found himself entrusted into his aunt's care, he had been understandably horrified.

After the banal gentility in which he had lived in Edinburgh, Waldo found Hebrides Hall, and the wilds of the island overwhelming.

His aunt, who was constantly shadowed by an irritable terrier named Fifi, had decorated the ancestral home with obscure paintings, exotic trinkets, and the skins—head included—of several strange animals. Even the servants of Hebrides Hall were peculiar. Aunt Phoebe's maid Dorothy was said to have "the sight", and plagued Waldo with her visions of imminent doom - visions which usually included Waldo meeting an imminent and tragic end.

At the age of eight, Waldo was granted an escape, when he was sent down to Eton to board. His relief at living amongst his peers was countered by the startling revelation that he wasn't as like them as he had assumed.

"Imagine being the heir to a woman!"

"It's nearly as bad as being the son of a barrister."

"Oh, did we make you cry, Lady Waldo?"

In Scotland, Waldo had always been sure of his status as "better", but down in England, amongst the sons of dukes, earls, and viscounts, he became acutely aware that this status depended upon to whom it was he was comparing himself.

He had never thought much on money or power, but in Eton, both these things were at the forefront of everyone's mind. Who was in line to the highest title? Whose father had amassed the most wealth? These two questions—and their answers—dictated the pecking order of life within the school, and Waldo soon discovered that he was perilously close to the bottom rung of that ladder.

As a practical child, Waldo knew that there was little he could do at present to remedy such matters, but he began in earnest to plot how he might—as an adult—overcome the difficult circumstances of his birth.

He needed money—of which the estate in the Hebrides provided little—and he needed power. In order to attain both these things, there was the only path that Waldo could take; that of the politician.

For the duration of his schooling, Waldo endeavoured to study hard and ingratiate himself with the right people. He increased his efforts doubly once he entered Oxford. By the time Waldo had finished reading the Liberal Arts, he had become an expert tuft-hunter and considered some of England's finest as his close companions.

"I don't understand the need to take up a position in Whitehall," Aunt Phoebe grumbled when Waldo returned to Hebrides Hall to pack for the final time.

"The need, my dear aunt," Waldo replied shortly, "Arises from your blatant mismanagement of my inheritance. If I am to accrue any fortune, I must do it myself."

"Perhaps not, dear nephew. When I was in In-jaaa—" Aunt Phoebe began, but Waldo cut her off with a wave of his hand.

"I could not give tuppence about your time in India, Aunt," Waldo interjected, "In fact, I never want to hear you mention India again."

"Suit yourself," Aunt Phoebe huffed, and the sound of the elderly Fifi's growling accompanied Waldo out the door.

The beginning of Waldo's career in politics coincided with the outbreak of revolution in France. As Waldo rose through the ranks of Whitehall, his diplomacy and tact—which mostly involved a lot of boot-licking—became noted.

"We need a man in Vienna, Havisham," Lord Ascot bellowed one morning to a beleaguered Waldo, "How's your French?"

"Exemplary, my lord," Waldo replied, most earnestly.

"Then pack your trunk, you'll sail in the morning."

Vienna was filled with aristocratic émigrés from Paris, all eager to find a way to overthrow the hoards of peasants who had so violently upset the status quo in the Kingdom of France. Waldo, equally as eager to play his part on behalf of Britannia and her King, threw himself into his work, only to fall at the first hurdle.

His French, which he had previously thought exemplary, was not up to scratch. In fact, it was nonexistent.

To remedy the matter, Waldo tried several approaches. He tried speaking very, very slowly, to better help the French understand his English. When that didn't work, Waldo tried speaking slowly and loudly, his voice often rising so high, that on numerous occasions he was accused of shouting.

Despite all his efforts at translation, the perfidious French still refused to understand him, not even when he added wild gesticulations to his words.

Waldo began to fear that his career as a diplomatic envoy would come to an abrupt end before it had even begun, until the night that he met Georgette.

The daughter of an impoverished comte, Georgette was elegant, beautiful, and—more importantly—bilingual. A hasty marriage was arranged, and within a week of making their nuptials, Georgette was assisting Waldo with making inroads with the locals. Waldo proudly arranged British military assistance for The Battle of Valmy—where the Austrians tried to overthrow the French regime and have Louis XVI restored to his throne.

Of course, it failed miserably, and the following year the king and his wife, Marie Antoinette, were beheaded. However, Waldo had no further care for that ghastly business, for he had already returned to England's shores with his beautiful bride.

And better yet, he had returned as a success.

True, many soldiers had perished in the battle, but what were a few lost men when Whitehall was so grateful to Waldo for having had Britannia play her part? So pleased were they that they awarded him a tidy sum for his great efforts. With his new fortune, Waldo purchased a seat in Parliament from one of the rotten boroughs, and the lease on a grand house on Grosvenor Square, where he and Georgette set up home.

After many years of longing, he had finally achieved both money and power. Just before summer, Aunt Phoebe sent word that she would be taking a tour of Ireland for a few months and that Waldo was welcome to bring his new bride to Hebrides Hall. As her letter coincided with Georgette's announcement that she was increasing, Waldo decided to take his wife back to Scotland, so that his son—for it would be a boy—might be born on the estate he would one day inherit.

Now, here Waldo was, in Hebrides Hall, with the son he hoped would achieve even greater things than he, a daughter he had not expected, and a vague hope that Aunt Phoebe might be kidnapped by Fenians and never return.

Sadly, Aunt Phoebe was not spirited away by rebel-rousing Irishmen, but even her return to Hebrides Hall could not distract Waldo from his newfound happiness; Sebastian.

His son was a bonny babe, with eyes so navy-blue that they could almost be mistaken for violet. His sister was similarly blessed, which was lucky, for it saved Waldo and Georgette the trouble of having to think of a name for the girl.

As babies, swaddled in blankets, it was almost impossible to tell Sebastian and Violet apart; both dressed in muslin gowns and caps upon their curly heads they were completely identical. After much confusion, Dorothy, in all her infinite wisdom, suggested dressing one in gowns trimmed with blue edging—a colour which was believed to ward off evil spirits—in order to tell them apart.

Waldo agreed, and while he did not believe in silly superstitions, he still made it clear that it was Sebastian who should wear the blue-trimmed gowns—just in case.

It was not that Waldo did not love his daughter; he did—it was just that he loved his son more. Sebastian was a being whom Waldo could mould to his own desire and who would proudly carry on the family name. While Violet…well, she might one day make a good marriage.

Waldo's preference was not noted by the twins in their early years, as they enjoyed an idyllic childhood roaming the wilds of the island. Neither seemed to notice that there was one gaping difference between them, nor, for a time, did they realise that they were actually two separate beings, so attached were they.

It was only when the time came to educate the pair that it dawned on Sebastian and Violet that their futures might take very different paths.

"Why can't I learn Latin?" Violet queried, on the morning of Sebastian's first lesson in the Classics.

"Latin is for boys, chérie," Georgette replied brusquely.

"But I want to learn Latin," Violet replied, with a petulant lip.

"Nobody wants to learn Latin," her mother clarified, with a faint shiver, "But Sebastian has to so that he will be at an advantage when he goes to Eton."

Eton?

Violet exchanged a startled glance with her brother across the breakfast table. No one had ever mentioned that they might one day be separated.

"I don't want to go to Eton," Sebastian spluttered, dropping his silver spoon with a clatter.

"Well, you have to," Georgette's patience was beginning to wear thin; she was not the maternal type and found time spent with her offspring exceedingly trying. "You will go to Eton, then to Oxford like your Papa, and then you will take up a position in government before you get married and inherit the title."

Again, Sebastian and Violet glanced at each other in surprise. How was it that Sebastian's life had been planned out so thoroughly without their knowledge or agreement? Did their parents not know that the twins had made plans of their own?

"I am not going to Eton, or Oxford, Mama," Sebastian replied, sticking out his chest importantly, "I will stay in Hebrides Hall and marry Violet."

To the twin's surprise, no admonishments sprung forth from their mother's lips. Instead, an amused giggle sounded out across the dining room.

"Ah," Georgette replied, bestowing a rare glance of affection upon her children, "I am afraid that you two getting married is not allowed. Besides, when the time comes, I can guarantee that neither of you will want to marry the other."

Not allowed? Violet gulped; if she was not allowed to marry Sebastian, then how on earth would she remain at Hebrides Hall? The wind-battered island, with its wild hills and turbulent seas, was the only place she wished to live.

"Then I will marry Papa," Violet shrugged, avoiding Sebastian's wounded gaze.

"I definitely think you won't want that, when the time comes," Waldo snorted, glancing up from his newspaper. "Now, run along, you two. Your mama and I want to finish our breakfast in peace."

Sebastian and Violet fled the table, muttering despairingly to each other about the injustice of life. But, as most children of five are wont to do, they forgot their troubles within a day, and there was no more talk of Eton from their parents, until the following year.

Anyone passing by Hebrides Hall, the night before Sebastian was set to depart, would have been forgiven for thinking that a dreadful murder was taking place, such were the howls.

"I won't go," Sebastian roared, tears streaking his porcelain face.

"I won't let him go," Violet added, her face flushed with agony.

"Neither of you has any say in this," Waldo answered, his shout the loudest of the three, "And if you don't stop your tantrum, I won't allow Sebastian to return at the end of Michaelmas."

The twins abruptly halted their protest, their despondent sniffs the only sound now filling the room.

"Good," Waldo gave the pair a stern glance, "Now, off to bed with you."

The children scurried to their bedroom, where the nursery maid attempted to soothe their battered souls as she dressed them for bed.

"You'll be reunited by the end of the year," Agnes chirped, as she tucked them under the coverlets.

"But that's forever away..."

"Tosh, it's just two months. Now, sleep."

The door clicked shut behind the nurse but within minutes it was opened again, and Dorothy, bearing glasses of warm milk spiced with nutmeg and ginger, appeared.

"What's this I hear about my two favourite children causing a ruckus?" she asked, placing the candle in her hand down upon the dresser, before handing the twins their drinks.

"They want to separate us," Violet whispered, before taking a sip of her milk.

"Separate you two?" Dorothy chuckled, "They might separate you by land and sea, but mark my words, you two will be joined forever."

"Really?"

"I'm quite certain."

"What do you see, Dorothy?" Sebastian, a great believer in Dorothy's supposed gift of the "sight", asked.

The old woman frowned as she gathered her shawl tighter around her dumpy form. Her eyes—Skye-blue, as the Scots called it—glanced from one twin to the other.

"I see two bairns, a boy and a girl, different in some ways, but so alike that they could be each other's mirror image," she said, before adding with a wink, "And I see mischief. Now to sleep with ye."

The door closed behind Dorothy, but as she had left her candle, light remained. Violet glanced at her brother, who was chewing his lip thoughtfully.

"That's it," he said, clicking his fingers as an idea manifested itself within.

"What's it?" Violet stifled a yawn; spiced milk never failed to send her to sleep—how clever Dorothy was.

"You shall go to Eton in my stead!"

The milk had lulled Violet into such a sleepy stupor, that she was too confused to offer her brother a reply.

"You shall dress as me," Sebastian continued, taking her silence for assent, "Then, once they see at Eton how brilliant you are, they'll allow you to stay and I can join you. We'll be together forever, then."

Sebastian had always been the leader of their duo; where Violet was quiet and shy, Sebastian was outgoing and loud. Where Violet was nervous and hesitant, Sebastian was determined and impulsive.

Her brother was such a force de jour, that even when Violet's common sense protested, she found herself being swayed by his enthusiasm, which is precisely what happened on this occasion.

"If you think it will work..?" she offered, hesitantly.

"Oh, I'm certain it will," Sebastian's eyes danced merrily, before their spark dulled somewhat, as they rested on Violet's head.

"There's just one thing..."

"Oh?"

"Your hair."

It was a testament to Violet's love for her brother that she did not weep that night, as he cut her hair with scissors stolen from the kitchens below. Even the next day, as she bid goodbye to her parents—dressed in Sebastian's clothes—she did not allow herself to cry.

"I don't know where your sister is," Georgette said with a huff, as she stroked—or believed she stroked—her son's cheek.

"She said that she could not bear to say goodbye," Violet replied, keeping her eyes lowered and her voice deep as she lied.

"Ah, my sweet prince, at least Mama is here," Georgette sighed, "Promise me you will write."

"Every day," Violet mumbled, as she fled her mother's hug for the waiting carriage.

"Au revoir, Sebastian!"

It had worked! Violet could not contain her glee, and as the carriage trundled along the road from Hebrides Hall toward Stornoway Harbour, where a boat would take her to Ullapool on the mainland, she let out a shout of glee. Everything was going to plan...

Unfortunately, her triumph was short-lived, for the moment before Violet was due to board the boat, a hand grabbed her shoulder and pulled her from the crowd on the dock.

"Not a word," Waldo cautioned, his face pale with anger.

Behind him, Violet spotted Sebastian, dressed almost identically to her in breeches and a tunic, worn under a green cloak. Her brother's face was stained with tears, and his hands were rubbing his bottom, as though it pained him.

"You," Waldo nodded at Violet, "Stay here. And you, Sebastian, get in line. And don't even think of attempting a grand escape. Your sister and I will stand here until your boat is safely out of the harbour and into the Minch."

Sebastian exchanged a tearful glance with Violet, before nodding silently and following his father's orders. Tears obscured Violet's view, as she stood beside her father and watched as the boat left the dock and the calm waters of the marina, to brave the frothy waves of the Minch.

"How did you know?" Violet queried, as her father led her back to the waiting carriage.

"There are certain things that girls do not do standing up," Waldo answered mysteriously, "And they most certainly do not do it in the flowerbeds."

This cryptic remark was not to be explained to poor Violet, who was returned to Hebrides Hall in disgrace. Both her actions and her hair brought great sorrow to Georgette, who declared herself done with her feral daughter.

"Send for a governess," Georgette wailed, "I need someone to take the child in hand. I cannot control her; she is too wild!"

That it was Sebastian, who was the wilder of her two children was not up for discussion. Violet's protests of innocence fell on deaf ears, and within a few weeks, she found herself imprisoned in the new schoolroom with Miss Thomas, a governess from the mainland.

Roaming the moors, clambering over rocks, or any kind of physical exertion was forbidden. Instead, Violet was permitted only to attend her lessons, practice her stitching in the parlour, or pick flowers in the garden. This would have been tolerable enough, was it not for the yawning chasm in Violet's heart.

She missed her brother.

When Miss Thomas supplied her with charcoal and watercolours for sketching, Violet found that her hand, almost of its own volition, began to draw her brother's face. Miss Thomas, who usually instructed Violet to draw kittens or daisies, was at first frustrated, until one particular day, she gave a frown.

"This is very good," she observed, as she glanced down at Violet's portrait of Sebastian, "Very good indeed."

As their ventures into embroidery, dancing, and flower arranging had met with little fruit, Miss Thomas decided to pursue Violet's burgeoning artistic talent. By the time that Sebastian arrived home, at the end of Michaelmas, Violet's sketching skills had come on in leaps and bounds.

Of course, no one took any note, given that Sebastian had returned with a glowing report from his Eton schoolmasters.

"My son is a genius," Waldo said proudly, from the head of the breakfast table, as he read the missive from the headmaster, "As I had suspected. Whoops—what's that I've spilt my tea on?"

"A portrait I drew for you, Papa," Violet whispered.

"Ah. Terribly sorry, dear. I'm sure you can draw me another one."

Violet felt hot tears prick her eyelids, and she might have burst out crying, had Sebastian not taken her hand.

"I cannot wait to see all your pictures, Vi," he whispered as he squeezed her hand in his.

And so, it was to be that the only member of Violet's immediate family who would ever think her a genius was Sebastian. Luckily, once Aunt Phoebe returned from a jaunt to the Isle of Man—with a taxidermy Fifi, whose long life had finally come to an end—Violet found another champion.

"The girl has talent, Dorothy," Lady Havisham said, as she held up one of Violet's paintings for the lady's maid to inspect.

"Did I not foresee greatness, when the bairn was born?" Dorothy appeared disgruntled that her own part in Violet's talent was going unrecognised.

"If I recall correctly, you foresaw a club-foot," Phoebe harrumphed, and the two ladies descended into gentle bickering. Once their argument had come to an end, it was somehow decided that Aunt Phoebe would pay for a drawing master to come from the mainland to nurture Violet's burgeoning talent.

"I don't think Papa will allow it," Violet said, knowing full well that he would not. Waldo would scoff at the very idea of lavishing any money on Violet when it could be spent on Sebastian.

"Oh," Aunt Phoebe's eyes glistened with amusement, "I don't think your father will remain here much longer to object. You see, since poor Fifi's departure from this world, I have been afflicted with an illness."

"An illness, Aunt?"

"Yes," Phoebe gave a definite nod of her head, "Homesickness. I fear my travelling days are behind me, and that I intend to take up residence in Hebrides Hall on a permanent basis. Something, I know, your father might find trying."

Indeed, once Phoebe declared that she was to stay, Georgette and Waldo made the quick decision to return to town.

"I am needed in Parliament," Waldo sniffed.

"And I am needed in Bond Street," Georgette winked.

"And what about your daughter?" Phoebe queried, her gaze steely.

"Well," Waldo blustered, "There's not much to Violet. And we're not expecting much of her. So—so—so we thought we'd just leave her here."

Her nephew's summation that there was "not much" to his daughter was enough for Phoebe to discern that it was time she took Violet under her wing. Lady Havisham drew up a list of all her notable friends—who were many— and each month, a new visitor arrived on the island, to help expand Violet's mind.

Along with these illuminating visitors, Aunt Phoebe arranged for painting lessons, new books, subscriptions to all the newspapers and periodicals, as well as granting Violet the freedom to roam the islands once more.

The years passed quickly, interspersed with visits from her parents from town, and summers with Sebastian on his break from school. Violet grew into a young woman with definite ideas and dreams, none of which, she knew, would marry with her parents' wishes for her future.

"Mama has written to say that she and Papa wish to take me to town for the little season," Violet said one evening, to Aunt Phoebe and Sebastian, who had returned for the island in August, once Summer-half had ended.

"She wishes me to make my come-out in the season proper, and hopes that I will secure a proposal by next May."

"A proposal?" Sebastian looked aghast, "Why on earth would you want one of them?"

"Well, one usually needs a man to propose before you have the banns read; otherwise, you look quite pushy," Aunt Phoebe replied mildly.

"Marriage?" Sebastian, again, looked aghast. Although the twins had long forgotten their youthful determination to marry each other, they had both longingly looked forward to spending more time together once Sebastian had served his time in Eton.

"Your father," Aunt Phoebe glanced fondly at Sebastian, "Expects you to go to Oxford and take up a position in Whitehall. He is less invested in your sister's future, but no doubt, he expects her to find a suitable husband who will take Violet off his hands."

"I don't want to work in stuffy old Whitehall," Sebastian groaned, "I want to be an actor. And, Violet has no wish to marry some damp-squib; she wishes to paint. To perfect her craft in Paris, and Venice, and Florence."

"If you were my children, I would allow you both to do as you please," Aunt Phoebe shrugged, "But as you are not, we must wait and see which way the wind blows. If Violet goes to town and finds a man that she would like to marry, then I will not stand in her way. On the other hand, if her father tries to force her down the aisle, I will be more than happy to stand in his way."

Violet was cheered by this thought; though her aunt was small in stature, she was quite wide and more than adept at brandishing her cane at anyone who dared cross her.

Aunt Phoebe decided to relocate from Hebrides Hall to London to assist with Violet's first season. She did not take up residence in Waldo's leased house on Grosvenor Square, preferring instead to re-open the family's townhouse on Jermyn Street.

It was in the house's cluttered drawing-room that Violet found sanctuary during her first few months as a debutante. There, she was free to paint to her heart's content, which helped to ease the anxiety of her most recent failure. Before coming to London, Violet had feared to get married—now that she was here, she was beginning to worry that she might be un-marriageable. She was asked to dance at Almack's by many eligible gentlemen, but few thought to repeat the request and none sought to call on her.

"I don't know what is wrong with the girl," Georgette wailed to Waldo, as the season neared its end.

"Perhaps we expected too much from Violet," Waldo offered, though he was hesitant to use the word "we", for he had never expected anything from Violet. Though his daughter was pretty enough, with an admitted talent for painting, she had no fortune which might entice a man to offer for her hand or make her stand out from the crowd.

A sensible marriage to a second, or third son would suffice for Waldo, and as Georgette's patience was beginning to wear thin, he felt that this might please her too.

Besides, there were other more pressing matters to which Waldo needed to attend.

"My dear," he cleared his throat, "I have been offered another position in Vienna. The government requires my diplomatic tact and language skills."

Georgette was forced to use all her diplomatic tact as she struggled not to snort with laughter at Waldo's remark on his language skills.

"Mmm?" she murmured, pressing her lips tightly together.

"Yes," Waldo drew himself up imperiously, "The war is at an end, and with Napoleon exiled on Elba, the four great powers of Europe will hold a congress to decide the continent's future. Viscount Castlereagh has personally requested that I attend."

"He has?"

"Yes," Waldo flushed, "And he has also offered me a generous pension, a knighthood, and a position for Sebastian if all goes to plan."

Georgette's eyes lit up at the thought of her beloved Sebastian being rewarded with a government position. She doted on her son, who was handsome, charming, and far easier to manage than her daughter.

"It is your patriotic duty to go," Georgette declared, "And as your wife, it is my duty to accompany you. My only concern is…Violet."

"Well…" Waldo cleared his throat again, "If she were going to make a fantastic match, she would have done it by now. We can leave her in Aunt Phoebe's care for a year or two, and perhaps some second son might snatch her up while we're gone. I fear you'll have to decide soon, Georgette, if you are to have a new wardrobe made up by the time of our departure."

A new wardrobe? Visions of balls and dances with various dignitaries and heads of states filled Georgette's mind, pushing out any concern for her daughter.

And so, it was decided that Waldo and Georgette would away to Vienna, leaving Sebastian and Violet in their aunt's care. Waldo attempted to strong-arm Lady Havisham into moving into the far more luxurious Grosvenor Square residence he had leased, but the old lady was recalcitrant.

"There is only one person in this room who is a peer in their own right," Aunt Phoebe growled, as she poked Violet's father in the stomach with the head of her cane, "And I think you'll find that's me. Sebastian and Violet will stay here, or they will stay nowhere at all."

Thus, it was decided that Violet and Sebastian would reside with their aunt in Havisham House, on Jermyn Street. Though this was only settled after the twins made two solemn promises. Sebastian swore that he would not set one foot inside The Gun Tavern, which was a noted hotbed for Revolutionary activity. And Violet promised that she would not seek the company of artists amongst the French refugees who resided in Grenier's Hotel at the top of the street.

"Ah, my dear Violet," Georgette sighed, as the time came to say their goodbyes, "How much I will miss you. Do take care of your brother. He is far more handsome than you, but I fear it has made him arrogant and liable to walk himself into trouble."

"Voyage sécurisé, Mama," Violet had replied, ignoring the veiled barb, "I promise that I shall keep an eye on him."

"And try to find a husband, dear."

"I shall," Violet promised, though she crossed her fingers behind her back as she did so. Love was not something that interested Violet, not now that she was finally free to live her life as she chose.

1 CHAPTER ONE

Wednesday was, in Violet's opinion, the most insufferable day of the week, for it meant one thing:

Almack's.

For three seasons, Violet had suffered through long evenings at the famed cattle-mart, inwardly marvelling at the repetitiveness of it all.

Every week, without fail, the patronesses of the much-vaunted assembly rooms provided their guests with stale cake, bitter lemonade, and dry conversation.

That vouchers for the ball were amongst the most coveted things in London seemed ridiculous to Violet, who found the event to be exceedingly dull. But then, she reasoned, she was not looking for a husband, and if one was marriage-minded, Almack's was the place to be.

As she trailed her aunt into the assembly rooms that evening, Violet found it crowded with flocks of white-dressed debutantes, each vying to glitter more brightly than the girl next to her. Meanwhile, well-dressed gentlemen roamed the room, speculatively eyeing their prey whilst braying loudly at each other. The girls in their dresses reminded Violet of sheep—fluffy and innocent, whilst the gentlemen put her to mind of wolves. Had she a pencil, Violet would have sketched a quick caricature, but alas one did not come to Almack's to draw--one came to find a husband.

It was a never-ending circle, Violet thought despondently, as she followed her aunt to their usual spot underneath the balcony. Young women blossomed like flowers each season and were plucked by the first gentleman to take a fancy to them, never to be seen again. Unless, like Violet, they were not plucked at all, and were forced to return each year to watch the whole charade play out, season after season.

Thankfully, Violet was not alone in being a weary perennial amongst a city full of bright annuals. As she and Aunt Phoebe approached the seats under the balcony—the unofficial seating place of wallflowers and chaperons—she spotted her good friend, Miss Charlotte Drew, already taking up residence on one of the chairs.

"La, Violet," Charlotte called cheerfully, "Fancy spotting you here."

"An utter surprise, I'm sure," Violet responded, as she deposited herself on the seat next to Charlotte.

Beside them, Aunt Phoebe clucked with disapproval at their dryness, though Violet rather thought she did it for show more than anything else. Her aunt had been tasked with doing her best to find Violet a beau, though thankfully Lady Havisham had decided her best consisted only of the bare minimum— escorting Violet to Almack's once a week.

Violet glanced across the room, where her other friend—Lady Julia—stood beside her parents, Lord and Lady Cavendish. Julia's parents were determined to find her a husband by the end of the season and were painstakingly intent on filling her dance card for the night. Thank goodness Aunt Phoebe was not so forward, Violet thought, as she observed Lady Cavendish push Julia forward to converse with a young man.

Above on the balcony, the orchestra struck up a tune, signalling the first dance of the night, and the trio fell into silence as they watched the familiar scene unfold.

"Is she?" Charlotte whispered in Violet's ear, a few minutes later, with a nod toward Lady Havisham.

Violet glanced affectionately at her aunt, who had drifted off to sleep on her chair. The ostrich feathers of her turban had slipped, to conceal her slumbering state from the room, and Violet thought it best to leave her.

"I once overheard her tell Dorothy that she always felt revived after a night at Almack's," Violet whispered to her friend, "Now I know why."

The two women giggled conspiratorially together and began to chat between themselves. There was much to discuss; Charlotte's father had recently delivered an edict that his eldest daughter must snare a duke, in order for Bianca—Charlotte's younger sister—to be allowed to make her come-out.

Violet, Charlotte, and Julia had, after much discussion, narrowed Charlotte's choice of available dukes down to one—the Duke of Penrith. He was one of the so-called "Upstarts", a trio of aristocratic friends who were renowned for their power and fortune.

"Thank goodness they never deign to set foot in Almack's," Charlotte said cheerfully, as she reached into her reticule to retrieve some biscuits, which she had wrapped in a handkerchief. Almack's offerings of refreshments were notoriously poor, and Charlotte quite often brought her own to stave off hunger during the long night. "I don't think I would have been brave enough to come tonight if I thought there was a chance I might run into Penrith so soon. I must prepare myself for battle before I attack!"

No sooner had Charlotte finished speaking, than the room erupted into furious whispering. Violet watched with interest as the assembled crowd turned their heads, almost as one, toward the door.

"Gosh," she muttered, accepting one the proffered biscuits with a smile, "I wonder if it's Prinny? I don't know why everyone gets into such a fuss about that man—he's a rake. And worse, he's a poor one. No Mama would think of allowing him to even look at their daughter if he wasn't a prince."

"Yes," Charlotte grinned in return, "But he is a prince, so he can do what he likes and still have the pick of the bunch."

Violet was about to argue that the reprobate regent could never have her, but then her eye caught on just who it was that the crowds were whispering about, and she suddenly lost her voice.

It was the Duke of Orsino; toweringly tall, fearsome, and one of the infamous Upstarts they had just been discussing. Violet gulped down her biscuit, worried that she might choke, for her mouth had gone suddenly dry.

She had seen Orsino once before, riding in the park and had thought him petrifying then. But here, in the sedate confines of the assembly rooms, he looked even more unnerving. He was tall of height, broad at the shoulder, and wore both these things with powerful, masculine ease.

Orsino commanded attention, though his green eyes were disdainful of all and sunder as they swept across the room.

For one, brief, second, his eyes locked on Violet's, and she felt a shiver of something—was it fear?—shake her body.

"Lud," Charlotte growled, through a mouthful of biscuits, "What on earth is he doing here? I thought the Upstarts never attended Almack's?"

"Eh?" Aunt Phoebe was awake now and peering—most blatantly—across the room. "Is that Orsino I spy? Must be in mind to find a wife, for I've never seen him here. Not once."

The other Mamas must have had the same thought, for they began to swarm around the duke in alarming numbers, and despite his height, Orsino quickly disappeared from view.

"Are you acquainted with the duke, Aunt Phoebe?" Violet asked curiously; her aunt was most unusual, in that she could claim acquaintance with a most varied array of people. Lady Havisham had dined with kings and criminals during her travels around the world, and she was oft quoted as saying that the latter were far more fun. If she were somehow acquainted with the terrifying duke, Violet would be far from surprised.

"Indeed, I am," Aunt Phoebe said, pulling her fox-stole—complete with head—around her shoulders, "I knew his late father. As a matter of fact, when I was in INN-JA—"

Violet felt her eyes glaze over as Phoebe began a long and detailed tale of her travels through India which, though interesting, had no relevance to the question she had just asked. Beside her, she heard Charlotte stifle a yawn, for she too had oft been treated to Aunt Phoebe's outlandish tales.

Both girls were so lost in trying to appear interested, that they did not notice two gentlemen approaching until they were standing right before them. And even then, Violet only noted their presence when their bulk blocked out the light from the chandeliers above her head.

Violet looked up to find none other than the Duke of Orsino standing above her, accompanied by a handsome gentleman, who though tall, was no match in height for the towering duke.

"Lady Havisham," Orsino gave a deep bow, his greeting directed at Aunt Phoebe, "How pleased I am to see you again."

Violet nearly groaned in dismay, as she noted the look of mischief in her aunt's eyes. Lady Havisham abhorred social niceties and was a firm believer in plain, Scottish speaking. If she sensed that someone was placating her in any way, she was not afraid to call them out on it.

In fact, Violet rather thought she enjoyed it.

"Poppycock. It is not I that you are pleased to see, Orsino, but my niece and her friend. Don't pretend you walked all the way over here just to speak to this old lady."

A part of Violet died a little inside, as her aunt added injury to the insult of her bald reply, by poking the duke very firmly in the gut with the head of her cane—which was shaped like a Highland cow.

"And who is this grinning addle-pate?" Aunt Phoebe continued, with a scowl to Orsino's companion, as Violet felt another part of her shrivel and die with embarrassment.

Nobody spoke to a duke in such a manner—even a fellow peer.

Violet stole a glance at Orsino certain that he would be livid at such rudeness, but to her surprise, she saw that he was trying not to laugh as he introduced his friend.

"This would be the Duke of Penrith," Orsino said, and Violet stifled a gasp. The haughty looking gentleman was none other than the duke whom Charlotte needed to snare—what were the chances?

Violet glanced at her friend, who was studiously inspecting the ceiling above her head, whilst her hands twisted nervously in her lap. For someone who had just had a much-needed prize land in her lap, Charlotte looked awfully glum.

Poor Cat, Violet thought; it was quite obvious that she found the prospect of "snaring" Penrith most unappealing. And Violet could not blame her; while his face was handsome, it wore a look of practised hauteur, and he held himself aloof, as though his presence there pained him.

"...Allow me to introduce my niece, Miss Violet Havisham, and her good friend, Miss Charlotte Drew."

Violet's attention was drawn back to the two interlopers, who offered both her and Charlotte courteous bows at her aunt's introduction.

To her surprise, despite Aunt Phoebe's outrageous tonoure, and the gaggles of eligible young misses eagerly awaiting their attention, Penrith requested that Violet and Charlotte grace he and Orsino with a dance.

Dancing with anyone—let alone a petrifying duke—was the last thing that Violet wanted to do, but in the name of friendship, she rose and accepted Orsino's proffered arm.

Gemini, she thought, as her hand made contact with a band of steel muscle; it was like touching a rock. A pair of questioning, green eyes met hers briefly, before looking away and Violet felt herself shiver once more. There was something so disconcerting about the duke, she thought, as he led her toward the dancefloor.

For his part, Orsino seemed entirely disinterested in her, avoiding her gaze as they waited for the current dance to come to an end. His posture was rigid, back straight as he scowled around the room at the curious faces who glanced at them.

"Do you like to dance, your Grace?" Violet ventured, for the silence was beginning to press on her.

"As much as the next man," Orsino answered curtly, his self-assured abruptness igniting Violet's Celtic temper.

"I'm afraid that does not really answer my question," she snipped, surprising herself at her boldness, "Unless I was to ask the next man if he likes dancing too. Perhaps you might tap Sir Dudley on the shoulder and enquire on my behalf, your Grace?"

Orsino glanced down at Violet, his expression rather startled. "I beg your pardon," he stammered, his green eyes finally meeting hers, "I did not mean to sound rude. I'm afraid that I do not get out much in polite society, and my repertoire is not what it should be."

"This is England, your Grace," Violet replied, "If you cannot manage witticisms, a comment or two on the weather will suffice. There's a reason why it's called small-talk."

"The weather?" Orsino raised a bushy brow, the eyes beneath now sparkling with interest. He was, Violet guessed, on the verge of smiling. His eyes crinkled at the corners and his lips twitched, as though he was suppressing a smile. It was strange that a man could look so fearsome one moment and almost adorable the next.

"Yes," it was Violet who now looked away, for a kaleidoscope of butterflies had taken up residence in her stomach. "It is a common feature in polite conversation. It looks like rain. It doesn't look like rain. If this rain does not let up, I'll eat my cravat. Et cetera et cetera."

She was blabbering, she knew, but the funny feeling in her stomach made it impossible for her to concentrate on what she was saying. Thankfully, the dance they were watching came to an end, and it was time for Orsino and Violet to take their place on the floor.

Violet said a silent prayer of thanks as she discovered that the next set was to be a Quadrille. The dance involved four sets of partners, and as such, she had to spend but a little of it with Orsino. When he did touch her—a clasped hand, or a touch on the small of her back as they changed partners—it made her feel most peculiar. Not to mention that when his eyes caught hers, and he half-smiled at her, she almost tripped over her feet.

When the music came to an end, Violet allowed her shoulders to sag with relief; her ordeal was over. That other ladies might covet the idea of dancing with an eligible duke did not cross Violet's mind—she simply needed to be away from Orsino and the queer feelings he inspired in her stomach.

"I apologise," Orsino said, as he came to claim her hand, "With all that dancing, I did not have a chance to discuss the weather any further. In my opinion, however, it does look like rain—et cetera, et cetera."

Violet frowned slightly in confusion; had he made a joke? She glanced up at him from the corner of her eye, saw that his easy smile had disappeared, replaced instead with a fearsome glare, and decided that he hadn't.

A man like Orsino did not jest, Violet thought, as she tried to quash the topsy-turvy emotions which threatened her equilibrium.

Orsino offered her his arm, and with the eyes of the room following their every move, led her from the floor toward Charlotte and Penrith.

Charlotte wore the look of a fox who had been encircled by a pack of hounds as she stood beside her own duke, and Violet felt a stab of pity for her friend who would be forced to pursue a man she quite obviously disliked. At least Violet might bid Orsino adieu and never have to set eyes on him again.

Charlotte gave a smile of relief as she spotted Violet approaching, and once Violet had reached her side, she determinedly linked arms with her friend.

"Well," Charlotte cried gaily, quite obviously glad to be on her way. "Thank you for the dance, your Grace. I am sure that there are a dozen other girls waiting in the wings to take my place."

"Yes, thank you," Violet echoed, her eyes nervously avoiding Orsino's gaze as she allowed Charlotte to lead—nay, drag—her away.

"Should you not try and engage Penrith further?" Violet whispered as she and Charlotte pushed their way through the crowd. Curious faces peered at them as they went, striving to catch a glance of the two girls who had managed to attract the attention of the two elusive dukes.

"Oh," Charlotte wailed, her face a picture of anxiety, "I know that I should, but I cannot. Not when he took me by surprise."

Violet felt a pang of sympathy for her friend, who seemed most overwrought. "Don't worry," she said reassuringly, "Men are strange creatures; Sebastian often says that when he thinks he cannot have something, he wants it even more. I'm sure that by making yourself unavailable, Penrith will tie himself in ribbons trying to get you."

Her words did not do much to soothe Charlotte's nerves; in fact, she seemed even more put-out by Violet's assertion. It was almost as though she did not wish to succeed at the plan they had earlier hatched. They soon reached the chairs beneath the balcony, and Charlotte threw herself down into her seat, with a sad sigh.

"Ladies," a voice called, quickly followed by the figure of Lady Julia, "Did my eyes deceive me, or were you both dancing with dukes in my absence?"

"We were," Violet replied, patting the seat next to her for Julia to sit down.

"My mama is in a quandary," Julia continued, her beautiful face near split in two with a mischievous smile, "She has spent the evening forbidding me from visiting the wallflower corner—as she calls it—and then the two most eligible men in the room decide that this is where they will pick their partners from. Needless to say, she sent me over to you both post haste, so that I might bask in your reflected glory."

"I would hardly call dancing with a snoot a glorious occasion," Charlotte grumbled, "Penrith has all the charm of condensation related damp."

"And Orsino is most fearsome," Violet added, not to be outdone, "'Twas like dancing with a particularly irritable mountain."

"I rather think that there is nothing wrong with a man who looks like he could wrestle a cow if he had to," Julia replied, giving Violet a knowing glance, as though she could see through her facade of indifference.

"Pray tell when might that particular occasion arise?" Charlotte queried with a laugh.

"One never knows," Julia shrugged and offered Violet a wink, "But if it did, would it not be grand to have Orsino there to protect you from a bovine-related catastrophe?"

Charlotte and Julia descended into gales of laughter, and Violet pretended to join them, though inside her heart was hammering a nervous tattoo.

There was something about the duke which made her feel most peculiar, and she was glad that she would never have to see him again.

As Charlotte and Julia chattered betwixt themselves, Violet experienced the strange sensation of feeling as though she was being watched. She turned her head and her eyes settled upon Orsino, who though chatting to Penrith, and another man Violet did not recognise, was glancing her way.

Her eyes met his, and she quickly looked away, as a pleasurable shiver made its way down her spine.

Orsino was dangerous, she decided firmly, as she turned her attention back toward her friends. And no level-headed woman would even think of entertaining any fantasies about him. But even as she had decided this, Violet felt her fingers twitch, and she realised that her hands were aching to put to paper the image of the man that was now emblazoned upon her mind.

Drat.

2 CHAPTER TWO

Gideon Michael Jack Pennelegion, the sixth Duke of Orsino, and Jack to his friends, frowned slightly as he considered his appearance in the mirror.

His valet, Johnson, whom he had inherited from his late brother, had insisted on tying his cravat in a complicated knot which had taken a half-hour to complete.

That the end result was the height of fashion was beyond doubt; what was doubtful was that Jack was at all taken by said end result.

"It's a bit…" Jack trailed off as he considered himself now from the side.

"Yes?" Johnson's tone was tetchy, for he realised in what direction his master's mind was headed.

"It's just a tad…"

"Yes?"

"Well, it's pink, Johnson. And not a little bit. Nor a tad. It's very, very pink."

"Campion rouge, your Grace," Johnson replied with a well-practised sigh, "Men are bashing down doors on Bond Street in an attempt to secure a cravat in that very colour."

"They are?" Jack did not quite manage to keep the tone of disbelief from his voice.

"They are." Johnson was definite.

"And," Jack continued, despite knowing he would exact the man's ire, "It's a little bit frilly."

"A little bit?"

"It's very frilly," Jack gave a sheepish grin, "I look like a macaroni. I know you said that the Waterfall knot was the done thing this week, but perhaps we might try something simpler—and in white."

Johnson gave another sigh and began to remove the offending garment, all the while muttering unintelligibly under his breath. Jack did not quite catch what it was that Johnson was saying, but he understood the gist of it. Even

20

more so, when he heard the wounded valet whisper his brother's name.

"You're correct," Jack said, startling poor Johnson from his mutterings, "It would have suited Frederick perfectly. And what's more, he would have been far more grateful for your efforts than I. But we must remember that Frederick is gone, Johnson. It is I you are dressing now, not he."

A hesitant sniff greeted this declaration, and Jack averted his gaze from his valet's watering eyes. There was a lump in his own throat, and if he were to see Johnson's tears, he might dissolve into blubbering himself.

Which would not do, for Jack Pennelegion never cried.

"He was a fine man, your Grace," Johnson finally said, clearing his throat as he began work on tying a fresh, white cravat, "So fashionable, elegant, and refined. A man such as he was so easy to dress."

"As opposed to a man like me?" Jack queried dryly, though he took no offence from Johnson's slip.

It was universally agreed that his brother Frederick had cut a very dashing figure. The papers had oft said that his stature and looks had been pleasing enough to give even Beau Brummell a run for his money. Tall, slim, and fashionably pale, the late duke had been the very epitome of male perfection—especially when contrasted with Jack.

Jack stood at over six foot three—so tall that his brother had once joked he ought to be measured in hands and not inches. His height, when coupled with his broad shoulders and muscular frame, gave the impression of a prize-fighter, or a manual labourer—not a member of the aristocracy.

To add further offence, Jack's skin was tanned from his years spent on the continent with the army. No amount of Olympian Dew or any other concoctions that Johnson tried to slather him with would ever make it pale again.

Which, Johnson often said, was a pity, for if Jack's dark locks had been coupled with alabaster skin, he just might have been able to pull off the look of a Romantic.

Though probably not. Most Romantics looked as though they might collapse under the weight of a quill, whereas Jack—like his good friend Lord Montague often said—was so large that a bull might baulk if challenged by him.

"'Tis perfect, Johnson," Jack said, once his gentleman's gentleman had finished for the second time.

"It's the Irish knot, your Grace," Johnson sniffed, with a modicum of distaste, "Simple enough to suit a Hibernian. Make of that what you will."

"I have never had any trouble with an Irishman," Jack laughed, as he allowed Johnson to assist him with shrugging on his coat.

"Then you probably haven't met many," Johnson muttered, as he brushed nonexistent specks of lint from his master's broad shoulders.

Once done, the older man took a step back to survey his work, gave a reluctant sigh and pronounced Jack ready.

"It will have to do."

"It will," Jack grinned, "For I cannot stand another minute's fussing, Johnson, and even if I could tolerate it, I wouldn't want to be late."

Jack grabbed his hat from the dresser and raced out the door, afraid that if he lingered any longer, Johnson might find something else to do—like cut his hair. The valet's eyes had been longingly glancing from Jack's curly locks to the scissors by the wash table, but Jack had no desire to submit to yet another shearing.

He was beginning to feel like a sheep, he thought, as he clattered down the stairs of Orsino Hall. Having a valet tend to his morning ablutions—not to mention his afternoon, evening, and night-times ones too—was not something that Jack thought he would ever become accustomed to.

He had spent much of the past decade in the army, serving under Wellington. First on the Peninsular, then in France, for the One Hundred Days War and the bloody battle of Waterloo.

Oh, he had been accompanied by a valet of sorts, but Higgins had been far more interested in making certain that Jack's musket and blade were in working order than worrying about his Captain's hair. And he had not followed the new duke back to London, when news of Frederick's death in a carriage accident reached Jack, claiming that he was unsuited to any life except an army one.

Jack, now having spent a year suffering under the trappings of dandified wealth, was inclined to agree; Higgins had but one eye, and he would have resented using it to assess the latest fashions.

Outside, a warm spring sun shone down on the stable-yard, where a groomsman hastily saddled up Ares, Jack's Arab hot-blood, whom he had purchased on his return to England.

"Is His Grace certain that he does not wish to take the carriage?" the groomsman queried, with a dubious glance to the sky.

"His Grace is quite certain," Jack replied dryly, still marvelling at how accustomed he had become to referring to himself in the third. There was not a hint of a cloud on the horizon, and even if there had been, Jack would have preferred to ride on horseback. He was a man of the outdoors, and would never choose a carriage—no matter that it was furnished with leather squabs and brocade curtains—over a good ride.

He mounted Ares with practised ease and, with a light hand, guided him from the stable yard. Outside, St James' Square was quiet and sedate as always, but within minutes, Jack was trotting down the busier Pall Mall toward Horse Guards' Road and Whitehall.

As he weaved expertly through the hoards of carriages and carts which clogged up the road, Jack's mind pondered over just why he had been summoned to the War Office.

Since his return, he had engaged quite frequently with certain ministers, offering advice on all matters military. He had risen from the position of Captain to General during his years of service, and as such had accumulated a vast wealth of knowledge on tactics and diplomacy. Not to mention that he had met, face to face, many of the politicos Britain was now bargaining with, in Vienna.

But, this particular summons had not come from any of the ministers with whom Jack usually dealt. No. It had come from a man by the name of Nevins, with whom Jack held no acquaintance at all.

When he entered the building of the War Office, Jack was directed to a small office on the uppermost floor, where a watery-eyed gentleman awaited.

"Your Grace," Nevins stood as Jack entered the room, nibbling nervously on a lip which was half concealed beneath a bushy moustache, "How good of you to come."

"Please," Jack frowned at the ceremony, "Call me Orsino."

"As you wish."

Nevins waved a hand to the chair before his desk, and Jack settled himself in. The older man made quite the show of closing the door to his office, before returning to his chair and glancing at Jack gravely.

"I have been tasked," Nevins began, after a minute of very serious staring, "With weeding out any spies who might have infiltrated Whitehall. Little birds have been singing in my ear about a certain someone in Vienna, who has been feathering his nest by providing information to the enemy."

"Lud," Jack blinked; espionage was not his usual remit. He could not understand why Nevins had summoned him, of all people, for this task, but then Nevins spoke again.

"I hear you're acquainted with the Honourable Mr Havisham, who is acting as an envoy for the Crown?" Nevins said, watching Jack from under hooded, cold eyes.

"Yes," Jack nodded; he had worked with Waldo Havisham during the Congress of Vienna. He was quite dry, as those political sorts tended to be, but he was accomplished at his job.

"We will instruct Mr Havisham, through coded letter, to find out what he can about this spy," Nevins continued, "I want this kept top-secret, so the letter must appear as if it came from a family member. Mr Havisham had offered his son's services as a translator, before he left," Nevins gave a sigh. "I don't suppose you could rope the lad in to help and have him write the missives in French—pretend they are for his mama, to throw anyone off the scent? And have him mention you, so Havisham knows who is instructing him. I don't see much coming from all this, but we must try."

Nevins went on to detail just what Jack needed to write in the letter and the code that he should use.

"This could all come to nothing," he said with a sigh as he finished, his bushy eyebrows drawn into a frown of annoyance. Nevins, Jack knew instinctively, was not a man who liked to waste time. This rather endeared him to Jack—despite his grumpy mien—for Jack was of a similar disposition.

"Indeed, it might not—but we must try," Jack replied, taking the sheaf of paper upon which the notes were scribbled and placing it in the breast pocket of his coat. "Nothing worse than a spy."

"No," Nevins blinked, "I don't suppose there is."

Their discussion now at an end, Jack took his leave. He mulled over Nevins' instructions, which had been vague, to say the least. Still, if a little bird had chirped in his ear that there was a spy lurking in Whitehall with links to Vienna, then they were obliged to act upon it.

With his meeting concluded far earlier than he had anticipated, Jack found himself at a loss as to what to do with the rest of his morning.

At home, there was paperwork and correspondence from his various estates which could occupy him, but Jack did not feel much like sitting in his library. If he was in the country, he might have taken Ares for a long ride to inspect his lands, but this was London, and open fields were few and far between.

On a whim, Jack decided to take a jaunt through Green Park, which was quite unfashionable, unlike its neighbour Hyde Park, where the bon ton sought to be seen parading along Rotten Row.

This unfashionable state was a merit in Jack's eyes, for it meant that the bridle paths were near empty and that he might enjoy his ride without scrutiny.

There had been many things with which he had been forced to become accustomed to when he had inherited the title, but the thing he struggled with most was his newfound notoriety.

As a second son, even to a duke, Jack had never garnered much interest from the ton. Perhaps, had he been more fashionable and less fearsome looking, he might have enjoyed some degree of fame. He could have taken his place as another well-heeled dandy after Oxford, but Jack had not wished to enter into society, preferring instead the camaraderie, adventure, and relative anonymity of the army.

After fate had forced him into the ducal seat, he soon found that his wish to live an undisturbed life would be more difficult than he had assumed. The papers detailed his every move; where he had been, with whom he had spoken, what lady he might choose to marry. It was galling for Jack, who truly believed that there were far more important things for the papers to discuss; such as the goings-on in Parliament, the riots up North, and the general poverty the country suffered under while their Prince Regent plundered the Kingdom's coffers.

In order to dissuade the papers—not to mention the sycophants and meddlesome mamas who hounded him at every outing—Jack had adopted a fearsome mien anytime he stepped out in public. When this scowl was coupled with his enormous stature, it had a most frightening effect, and soon the papers were referring to him as the Duke of Thunder, whilst meddlesome mamas gave him a wide berth.

This suited Jack perfectly; allowing him breathing room to become accustomed to the new duties and responsibilities which came with the title. It also offered the added bonus of not having to worry about having a dozen debutantes thrown at him each time he stepped outside the door.

Debutantes now fled at the mere whisper of his name, he thought with no little pride.

As Jack cantered along the bridle path which ran along Constitution Hill, he found his mind drifting back to the previous night and a pair of violet-blue eyes.

Miss Violet Havisham had not been cowed by him, rather the opposite in fact. She had seemed to enjoy setting him down for his abominable rudeness, much like her spirited aunt.

Jack recalled, with a slight pang, his idiotic behaviour the night before. He had not been trying to play the Duke of Thunder with Miss Havisham and scare her with his silence—rather the opposite. He had been captivated by her eyes—so blue, they were almost violet—and bowled over by her nymph-like beauty.

The trouble with Jack was that, unlike his two friends—but especially Montague—he had not had much experience with women.

Or any experience, if truth be told.

When confronted with Miss Havisham's unusual beauty, Jack's tongue had become inextricably tied, and his body had felt larger and more cumbersome than usual.

She probably thought him an oaf, he decided reluctantly, and he could not blame her.

Ahead Jack spotted two riders approaching, a lady sitting side-saddle, accompanied by her groom. As they approached, he slowed down, for he recognised the lady.

"Lady Olivia," he called, as he brought Ares to a halt.

Lady Olivia was his late brother's fiancée, a charming young woman of four and twenty. As a couple, she and Frederick had been much celebrated by the papers as a most fashionable pairing. Indeed, today, Lady Olivia, despite wearing mourning blacks for her recently departed brother, looked as though she had stepped straight out from a fashion plate.

"Your Grace," she inclined her head regally in greeting, "What a pleasant surprise."

Despite her words, Jack guessed that their chance encounter was anything but pleasant for the young lady. A fit of honour had inspired Jack to offer for Lady Olivia's hand soon after he had assumed the title, and while her parents had been most eager for this new match, the lady herself was rather reluctant. Her father, Lord Cardigan, had been at pains to persuade Jack to wait, as his daughter was simply mourning first Frederick, and then later her brother. But as the months slipped by, Jack was more and more certain that Lady Olivia's reluctance had very little to do with mourning and more to do with a complete disinterest in Jack.

Not that he minded; he had simply suggested the marriage for it was the right—and convenient—thing to do.

Today, however, Jack felt a slight jolt of fear that Lady Olivia might soon decide she did desire to become his duchess. This fear was inspired by the memory of a pair of bewitching violet eyes and the longing they inspired within his heart.

"Well," Jack cleared his throat as a feeling of awkwardness stole over him, "I wouldn't like to keep you from your ride."

Lady Olivia smiled with relief, before bidding Jack goodbye in much cheerier tones than those with which she had greeted him. Indeed, Jack felt a similar lightness as he rode away from the woman he had once thought he should marry.

As he continued on his ride, Jack felt the letter from Nevins burning a hole in his breast pocket. The instruction to include young Mr Havisham in his mission felt almost like a sign from above. Jack was not usually given over to superstition. However, as his stomach fluttered pleasurably at the memory of Miss Havisham's bewitching eyes, he decided that there was always a first time for everything.

He would seize this opportunity to get closer to Miss Havisham, and he would battle valiantly against any obstacles which stood in his path. The biggest one being, he reluctantly conceded, himself, and his complete and utter lack of charm and romance.

.

3 CHAPTER THREE

A day of duty had left Violet feeling rather tired. It had begun by paying morning calls with her aunt to various society hostesses, while its end had involved a musicale, featuring several dreadful performances given by the many daughters of Sir Rupert Gideon. Each daughter was, it was whispered by the pained guests, even less talented than the last.

There was much relief all round when the performances came to an end as the clock struck eleven. Aunt Phoebe and Violet made straight for their carriage but were delayed by a crush of people similarly seeking to escape, lest anyone called for an encore.

It was just after midnight when the pair returned to Havisham House, and Aunt Phoebe declared that she would retire to bed at once.

"Don't stay up too late, dear," she instructed her niece, as she traipsed up the stairs, followed by Dorothy, her faithful lady's maid.

"I won't," Violet replied, though they both knew she was fibbing; Violet was, like a cat, nocturnal in nature.

Once she heard the door to Lady Havisham's bed-chamber bang shut, Violet stole into the cluttered drawing-room, which was cast in darkness. The dying remnants of a fire lingered in the grate, but after working the bellows for a few minutes, Violet managed to bring it back to life.

She lit a taper from its flames, and traipsed around the room, lighting what candles she could find. Some fine homes—like Charlotte's—had been fitted with newer gas-lights, but Havisham House would not be the recipient of such modern advancements whilst Aunt Phoebe was at its head.

Not that Violet particularly minded, she was quite taken by the romance of candle-light; it made it easier for her to imagine herself in a Parisian garret, or a Venetian Palazzo, or anywhere else rather than London.

Violet then threw open the heavy curtains, to allow moonlight to flood into the room and onto her easel. She had been working on a portrait of Aunt

Phoebe, in the style of Marguerite Gérard, and her fingers had itched all evening to return to her work.

She quickly donned an apron, to cover her dress, and began setting out paints on her pallet. She often worked at night; while the light was not what it should be, the peace of the house allowed her to become completely absorbed in her work.

Violet picked up a brush and began working in detail on Fifi, whom she had placed at Aunt Phoebe's feet. She could not say how long she was painting for—it might have been hours—when a noise from outside made her look up. It was Sebastian, clambering down from a carriage. She heard him give cheery thanks to the driver of the hackney and watched as he alighted the front steps of the house.

Curious as to the reason for his nocturnal visit, Violet placed her paintbrush down and rushed out to the hall to greet him.

"Why are you calling so late?" she whispered as she ushered him inside. Sebastian, having finished at Oxford, had taken up residence in gentlemen's lodgings close to Covent Garden. The rooms were funded by the small annuity bestowed on him by Aunt Phoebe, and though they were not so grand, they allowed him freedom that Violet envied.

"I needed to speak with you," Sebastian whispered, his eyes—a mirror image of Violet's own—alive with excitement.

"What on earth is so important that it could not wait until the morning?"

"My life-long dream, that's what."

Violet experienced a sinking sensation in her stomach as she followed her brother back into the drawing-room, acutely conscious that something startling was about to be unveiled.

"Violet," Sebastian said, once she had shut the door behind her, "I have been offered the lead-part in a production of Hamlet, which is to be staged in Newcastle."

"W-what?"

"I know," Sebastian nodded, mistaking her shock for awe, "It's quite the part. I can't tell you how pleased I am."

"But you cannot disappear to Newcastle," Violet argued, as she realised that her brother was not jesting but deadly serious. "Nor can you become an actor. Papa would take an apoplectic fit if he believed you were even thinking of treading the boards."

"Don't you think I know that?"

A scowl marred Sebastian's handsome face; their father's obsession with Sebastian's future was an even greater burden to shoulder than his disinterest in Violet. Waldo was determined that his son would follow him into politics and make something of the family name, despite Sebastian never having expressed an interest in the life of a politico. Waldo would not be best pleased if he were to find out about this venture into the arts.

"I will use a stage-name," Sebastian continued, his words gushing forth, as though he had been holding them inside for quite some time. "And no one shall recognise me up North. I just need your help, Violet, to hide my absence from Aunt Phoebe."

Violet sighed; she had known this midnight visit would shake up her well-ordered life. She also knew that no matter what she said, she would not be able to dissuade Sebastian from his chosen path.

A fire had been lit inside her twin brother, and as one who had known him his whole life—and even before that—Violet instinctively understood that the tempest brewing within Sebastian would consume him unless it was allowed to blow itself out.

"Please," Sebastian pleaded, imploring Violet with wide, hopeful eyes, "This is my one chance. You know how much I adore the stage; I want just one opportunity to live out my dream."

Violet knew full well what it was like to dream of a different life, and felt a stab of pity for her twin though this pity was not so great that it overruled common sense.

"How will I explain your absence to Aunt Phoebe?" she asked, though Sebastian must have taken her question for acquiescence, for his handsome face broke into a smile.

"It shall be easy enough," he promised her, "Just tell her I called when she was out."

It was a simple but perfect plan, Violet conceded, for Aunt Phoebe was always out.

"It will just be for a few weeks," Sebastian continued, as he sensed Violet's hesitation, "And no one else shall ask for me. I don't run with the sets who frequent White's and Boodles'. There will be no gossip columns to comment on my absence."

This was true; Sebastian's circle were not the type to pay morning calls or enquire into his whereabouts. Most of them had probably not seen the morning in many years. There would be no one to note her brother's absence apart from Violet and Aunt Phoebe—and the latter was so scatterbrained that it could take her a year to note that her great-nephew was missing.

"When I return, I promise that I shall put my head down, Vi, and begin working my way into Whitehall. I just need one last hurrah, before I surrender my soul to bureaucracy."

The sincerity in Sebastian's voice was most believable, though Violet could not tell if it was genuine, or down to his superb acting skills. Still, there had been no need for him to deliver such an earnest speech, for she had already decided she would support him.

"I couldn't care tuppence if you never make it to Whitehall, Sebastian," she replied with a smile, "Just promise me that you will take care of your person; Mama will never forgive me if she returns to find you harmed in any way."

"They use wooden swords in the theatre, Vi," Sebastian grinned, "Have no fear that I will return maimed."

"Just promise me you will return," Violet prodded her brother sharply in the chest, "I will miss you terribly."

"And I you," Sebastian gave a charming, lob-sided grin, "And when I inherit, I shall send you off to Paris, Violet, so that you might learn from the masters. I swear on my life that I shall."

Tears pricked Violet's eyes at his words; if there was one person in the world whom she believed cherished her dreams as much as she did, it was Sebastian.

"Oh, you silly addle-pate," Violet sniffed, as she reached out to pull her brother into a hug, "You do say the nicest things."

After a quick embrace, which involved lots of sniffing on Violet's part, Sebastian made to take his leave.

"I need to pack," he said decisively, when Violet objected, "Not to mention rest. We depart at the crack of dawn."

"Write to me, if you can," Violet said, as she walked Sebastian back to the door.

"There won't be time," Sebastian offered Violet a winning smile, "I shall be back before you even have the chance to notice that I am gone."

On this optimistic note, Violet bid her brother goodbye, her spirits buoyed by his belief that no one of note might look for him.

Unfortunately, only the next morning, Violet's cheerful outlook vanished with the arrival of an order from Whitehall, written by the duke she had tried valiantly to forget.

Mr Havisham,

Your father has volunteered your services as a translator for a very delicate task. I will call at your aunt's house tomorrow night to discuss further your service to the Crown. Do not breathe a word of this to anyone. If all goes well, I hope that I might be able to secure you a position in Whitehall when we are done.

Faithfully,

Orsino

Violet paled as she finished reading the missive, her mind instantly conjuring an image of the dark and forbidding duke. Dash Sebastian, she thought, as she curled the letter into a ball and flung it in the empty grate. For three years, he had pranced about London playing the dandy, and now that something was finally required of him, he had vanished.

Vanished with your blessing, a voice in Violet's head reminded her sternly.

Violet sighed. She had agreed to help her twin live out his dream; she could not now be angry with him for events which neither of them had anticipated. Violet crossed the room and fished the crumpled page from the grate. She smoothed it out and read it again, though her hands shook as she held it.

This was no laughing matter; Sebastian's future hung in the balance. If he did not assist Orsino with this task, he might be labelled as just another feckless young-blood and might never be offered another opportunity again.

Not to mention that when her father heard of Sebastian's failure, there would be a price to pay.

Violet thought on Sebastian's sincerity when he had promised to send her to Paris. Her twin would, if the roles were reversed, think of a way to make things work. It was only right that Violet do the same.

But how on earth could she make Sebastian appear from thin air? Violet bit nervously on her lip as she pondered the question; she was eager, but she was no miracle worker. As she set the letter down to rest on the mantelpiece, Violet caught sight of her reflection in the mirror.

People often noted how alike the Havisham twins were, despite the obvious difference of their sex. Their height, their colouring, and their striking eyes were perfectly identical. Even their faces were similar; in fact, Sebastian often bemoaned his elfin looks, thinking them feminine.

What a pity I do not have a beard, Violet thought, then stilled as an idea struck her.

It's preposterous, she told herself, but as she glanced down at the menacing letter again, she began to wonder if her idea might just be foolish enough to work…

4 CHAPTER FOUR

Havisham House was unlike any other home that Jack had ever visited. When he knocked, after nine o'clock on Friday evening, the door was opened, not by a servant, but by Sebastian Havisham himself.

"Your Grace," the young man greeted him in a low voice—as though he were afflicted by a cold—before ushering him into a darkened hallway.

Exotic paintings lined the walls, depicting far off lands and strange peoples, whilst a spicy scent permeated the air. Pieces of taxidermy littered the hall; a stuffed fox here, a macaw there, whilst an enormous stags' head was mounted upon the far wall.

"Lady Havisham herself shot that beast," the young man said, as he caught Jack peering at it.

"I don't doubt that she did," Jack commented, thinking on the wily Scotswoman. He could well picture her leading a hunt and petrifying any creature who dared cross her path.

"Would you—" Havisham hesitated, shifting uncomfortably from one foot to the other, "Would you like tea, or shall we get straight down to work?"

"Tea?" Jack allowed himself a bark of laughter, "Will you be serving it in the drawing-room with iced fancies and a lesson on needlepoint? Lud, man! The library will do—and something stiffer than tea, if you have it."

Young Havisham flushed beneath his beard, leading Jack to regret his teasing. He forgot, sometimes, that he was a duke, and that his words now carried more weight than they had before.

"This way, so," Havisham said, beckoning Jack down a dark corridor.

Parts of Havisham House were so ancient that they might have been medieval; Jacks' head was in danger of brushing off the ceiling, and several times he had to duck to avoid a low beam. There were some houses which had escaped the Great Fire of London, and Havisham House, Jack guessed, was one of them.

As well as being ancient, the house was tremendously dark—as though Lady Havisham wished to save on tallow. Sconces lined the walls but the candles within burned low and did little to alleviate the shadows.

"Here we are," Havisham said, as he opened a door into the library, though it was unlike any Jack had ever seen before.

It was lined by shelves of books, as one would expect, but Lady Havisham appeared to have collected so many works that she had run out of space. Books were piled upon the floor, in towering stacks which threatened to fall over at the slightest touch.

"Er, try not to knock off any of them," Havisham said apologetically, "You might be buried alive if you do."

The young man lightly picked his way across the cluttered floor, with Jack following, until he reached a small desk beside the fireplace. Within the grate, a small fire burned, and in this light, Jack was able to assess Havisham properly.

He was of smallish height and slight build, though he had tried to disguise this with padding at the shoulders. Valets across London, Jack knew, often stuffed their masters' shirts—and even their breeches—to make them appear more muscular, so he found nothing odd in this.

Havisham's hair, which was dark like his sister's, fell slightly over his eyes, and his young face was concealed by a beard. Facial hair was not much in fashion, but Jack supposed when a man was as elfin as Havisham, he might forgo fashion for the sake of appearing more masculine.

It was only when Havisham glanced up at him that Jack noted the true similarity between the young man and his sibling.

"Gracious," he said, despite himself, "Your eyes are so like your sister's."

"Well, we are twins," Havisham grumbled, averting his violet orbs away from Jack, "Though as I was born first, you might say that her eyes are like mine."

Twins? Jack blinked; he had not known Miss Havisham was a twin, though the similarity between brother and sister made more sense now.

"Of course," Jack nodded, "Forgive my surprise, but the similarity is uncanny. Shall we have a drink and get down to work?"

"A drink?" Havisham bit the lip beneath his bushy moustache nervously, "Of course. One moment, I will see what we have."

The young man rummaged through one of the drawers in the desk, eventually pulling out a very dusty bottle of cognac and two glasses. He hesitated, as though thinking before he poured Jack an enormous measure and a similar sized one for himself.

"Chin, chin," he said, raising his glass in a toast to Jack, before tossing it back in one go. Jack winced, as Havisham began to splutter and cough, spraying alcohol down his shirt and vest.

"Steady on, old chap," Jack said, as he took a mild sip of his own drink, "We have work to do."

Havisham nodded as he took out a handkerchief from the breast pocket of his coat and wiped himself down. Beneath his beard, Jack could see that his cheeks were once more flushed, and he felt a stab of pity for the young man. He was obviously nervous and appeared to think that he needed to impress Jack with displays of masculine bravado.

"I'd like to offer my thanks for your agreeing to this task," Jack said gruffly, hoping a few kind words might settle the lad. "You weren't obliged to, and it is much appreciated."

"Oh," Havisham gave a nervous smile in return, "I am more than happy to do my duty—though I still don't quite know what that will entail."

"Well, allow me to illuminate you," Jack replied, placing the glass in his hand on the desk and reaching into his pocket for the scribbled instructions from Nevins.

In a low voice, he explained what they needed to do; the letter was to be addressed to Havisham's mother, written in French, and the first letter of the first word in each sentence should spell out their coded message.

"Lud," Havisham scratched his chin, thoughtfully, "This might take a while."

"I have all night," Jack shrugged, as he placed himself in the chair opposite the desk, "Just make sure that the message instructs your father to send word at once about any dark rumours which concern members of the British delegation."

"As you wish," Havisham replied, as he reached for a quill.

Silence fell between the men, and for a time, the only sound that filled the room was the scratching of Havisham's quill against the page. Jack relaxed back into his chair, content to sip upon his brandy and wait. He cast his eyes around the library, idly admiring the various ornaments and trinkets which lined the shelves. He squinted curiously at some wild and hairy oddity and was just wondering if it was another piece of taxidermy when it suddenly sprang to life and jumped into his lap, hissing angrily.

"What on—" Jack cried, as he sprang to his feet and tried to extricate the claws—of what he now saw was a cat—from his breeches.

The feline, which looked so feral it might have just roamed in from the streets, clung on for dear life, hissing and scratching. It was only with a Herculean feat of strength that Jack managed to prise him away, and when he did, the impertinent thing did not even have the manners to run away. Instead, it set itself in front of Jack, glowering at him through narrowed eyes.

"Well, you are quite the beast," Jack muttered, with grudging respect, as he sat back down. He leaned over to idly stroke the cat's head, but another angry hiss had him hastily rethink that idea.

"That's Bagpipes," Havisham said fondly, glancing up from his work, "He's really a dear, once you get to know him."

"I'm sure," Jack replied doubtfully; the idea that the beast before him could ever be considered in anyway darling was quite unbelievable.

"No, really he is," Havisham said defensively, "He's just wary of strangers. I—I—My sister found him as a stray in Hyde Park; he was missing half an ear and almost starved. She's very fond of Bagpipes."

"Indeed?" Jack's interest in the cat piqued, now that he knew of its association to Miss Havisham. That the girl could love a beast as irritable and mangy as old Bagpipes gave Jack pause for hope. Perhaps she might be able to see past his own frightening exterior, to the man within.

"Ah," Jack cleared his throat awkwardly, hoping that he did not sound too obvious. "How is your sister? I had the pleasure of making her acquaintance at Almack's just the other evening."

Havisham paused but did not look up from his work.

"Violet?" he asked, after a long delay, "She is well enough. I would tell her that you asked after her, but I suppose as this is meant to be a top-secret endeavour, that it would be best if I did not."

"No!" Jack flushed, for his response had almost been a shout, "I mean, there is no need to keep the fact that I called a secret. You can say I called about a horse or some other such nonsense. Er, so you might tell Miss Havisham that I enquired after her if you wish."

"I might," Havisham said vaguely, dipping his quill into his ink-pot with far more vigour than necessary.

It was clear that the young man had no further wish to discuss his sister—a fact that Jack attributed to brotherly concern—but still, Jack could not resist pushing him further.

"Is she at home?" he asked, striving for nonchalance, but falling far short. To disguise his reddening cheeks, he stood up and strolled toward the mantelpiece, where he picked up an ornament to fiddle with. He was usually much more adept at hiding his emotions—a skill which often helped him win at cards—but when it came to Miss Havisham, he found that he could not conceal his nerves.

"Is who at home?"

Again, Havisham was obtuse, and Jack got the definite feeling that the young man did not wish at all to discuss his sister with him. Which irked Jack; he was a duke. True, he was not as suave and mannered as some gentlemen, but he did hold one of the highest peerages in the realm.

"Miss Havisham," Jack tried not to growl with frustration.

"I expect so," Havisham shrugged, his eyes still on his page.

Silence fell between the men and the only sound to be heard was that of Havisham's quill scratching on the page. Jack was at a loss as to what to do next. He had expected to be able to tease a few titbits about Miss Havisham from her brother, but he was meeting with a brick wall. A very stubborn brick wall.

After a moment's silence, Jack decided that a direct approach was what was required.

"I was quite charmed by your sister," he said bluntly, "If truth be told."
Havisham, who had been dipping his quill into the inkpot, knocked the glass jar over in surprise. The black ink began to spread across the table, and Jack rushed forth to mop it up with his handkerchief.

"She is a very beautiful young woman," Jack continued, determined that Havisham's little accident would not distract from his mission.

"Violet?" Havisham queried, rather stupidly, "You think Violet is quite beautiful?"

"Yes," Jack nodded, the tips of his ears burning as Havisham emitted a high, girlish giggle.

The young man cleared his throat, his cheeks as flushed as Jack's own. He averted his eyes back to his work and gave a Gallic shrug.

"Did you know that she's completely bald at the front?" he blurted out suddenly.

"I—what?" Jack blinked in confusion.

"Yes," Havisham gave a mournful sigh, "There was an incident with a candle a few years ago, and that patch of hair never grew back."

"I can't say that I noticed," Jack replied, casting his mind back to the night of his dance with Violet. He had not noticed anything odd about her hair—though perhaps she had had a piece fashioned for her.

"Oh, yes," Havisham continued cheerfully, "She can put one to mind of a boiled egg if you spot her in the right light."

Really! Jack had one sister, Lady Iris Lloyd, and he knew that he would never speak of her in such a manner to a potential suitor—even if he was being protective. Not least because Iris would skin him alive if she found out.

"My own father went bald at five and twenty," Jack shrugged, "As a potential future egg myself, it would be rather hypocritical to take umbrage with a small bald patch. Besides, your sister is more than just beautiful, she is…"

Jack trailed off; he did not have the vocabulary to put into words just what it was about Violet Havisham that had so entranced him. Her eyes, her face, her fine figure—all these things had, of course, been pleasant to behold. But there was more; a spark of fire when she challenged his manners, the humour in her smile. Even the ugly cat sitting by the table, whom no-one else might love, was a testament to a soft heart. There was so much more to Miss Havisham than just a pretty face, and Jack did not want to do her a disservice by waxing lyrical about her looks.

"She is..?" Havisham prodded him.

"Interesting," Jack smiled; that would have to do.

Havisham hesitated, as though he wished to push him further. Then, he evidently decided against it, for he returned to his work with a shrug.

"Violet is quite the dedicated spinster," he said, after a spell, "I fear that her only love will always be her art, your Grace. I should not like to give you hope, for I fear it would be false."

If his comment was meant to dissuade Jack, it had the opposite effect. Havisham's declaration that his sister was a determined spinster could mean only one thing; no one else had managed to capture her heart. If there was one thing that Jack loved, it was a challenge, and the idea that he might be the man to finally win Miss Havisham stirred something deep within his belly. "We'll see," Jack replied, his mind already plotting as to how he might instigate himself into Miss Havisham's affections.

An irritable sigh accompanied Jack's answer, and when he glanced up, Havisham was scowling at the page as he wrote. The lad was stabbing his quill so violently, that Jack feared he might end up tearing the paper.

"How goes it?" he asked, with a nod to the letter. He had much experience with angry men, and he realised it was time to move the subject away from Violet Havisham—no matter how much he might wish to linger on it.

"Nearly done. I just need to finish this line, then I will read back to you what I have written."

Jack waited patiently for a few minutes, as Havisham finished up his work. Once he was done, the young man read back to Jack—in a halting voice— what the secret code said.

"Good work," Jack grinned; the boy had got it in one. He had thought that he might be there all night, but only an hour had passed since his arrival.

"What now?" Havisham queried, as Jack took the letter from his outstretched hand.

Jack slowly fanned the page in the air, wanting to be certain that the ink was dry before he folded it.

"I will deliver this to a messenger, who will set out at once for Vienna," he replied, once he was certain that the ink had dried, "Once I have your father's response, I will call again."

"That might take weeks," Havisham gave a sigh that sounded somewhat relieved.

"Yes," Jack frowned; he had not gleaned as much information on Miss Havisham as he would have liked. Nor, had he managed to get her brother onside—rather the opposite, in fact. It would not do.

"I may have other things I need help with," Jack said quickly, keen to leave the door open should he need to return, "If you wouldn't mind?"

"Glad to help."

Havisham sounded anything but glad, but Jack ignored this and offered the lad a cheerful smile, before declaring that he must leave.

"My thanks again, for your help," he said, as Havisham led him back down the darkened hallway toward the door. Many of the candles in the sconces had burned out, indicating that he and Jack were the only people about at this late hour.

For a moment, Jack thought longingly of Miss Havisham, asleep upstairs. He imagined stealing into her bedroom and slipping under the coverlets beside her, and—

"Well, here we are!"

Havisham's voice, which sounded high-pitched and strained, interrupted Jack's thoughts. Which was merciful, for the idea of Miss Havisham in bed was the most exquisite of tortures.

"Until we meet again," Jack held out his hand, and after a moment of hesitation, Havisham took it. The young lad flinched a little, as Jack gave him a bone-crushing handshake—mild retribution for his earlier evasiveness. Jack strolled out the door, donning his hat, but before he descended the steps to his waiting carriage, he paused, momentarily overcome by mischief.

"Give my regards to your sister," he called over his shoulder.

The sound of the door slamming was the only response Jack received—though it must have been because Havisham had not heard him, for no-one would dare slam a door on a duke.

After delivering the letter to the messenger, who awaited him in the Horse Guards' building, Jack found himself at something of a loose end. The night was still young, by London standards, and should Jack wish to, there were a dozen balls, musicales, or other social gatherings which he might drop into. The idea of mingling with toplofty hosts and hostesses held little appeal however, for even when he was in an affable mood, Jack was no social butterfly.

Still, he did not wish to return home, where only an empty bed chamber and his own thoughts awaited. Seeking some sort of company—even if it was just that of the elderly Major Charles, who spent most nights asleep in his chair—Jack set forth for White's.

The club was quiet, as he had expected; the young bloods would be out gallivanting, whilst the married gentlemen had probably been strong-armed by their wives into socialising. Jack cast his eye around the drawing-room and spotted Major Charles, asleep in his chair by the fireplace. Another body, seated by the famed bow window, caught his eye, and Jack gave a cry of surprise.

"Montague," he called, as he tread a path toward his friend, "What are you doing here? I thought you'd be out trying to woo your fair Rosaline."

"Mmm?" Lord Montague glanced up, his eyes slightly glazed as though he had been lost in some very deep thoughts.

Which was a preposterous idea, for the rakish lord preferred to splash in the shallow end of the pond when it came to philosophising.

"I asked why on earth you're here?" Jack waved around the near-empty room as he slipped into the seat opposite Montague. "Surely there are more exciting places that London's most notorious bachelor might be found?"

Jacks' words were meant as a jest; Montague had a reputation as a charmer, and his female conquests—be they real or imagined—were oft hinted at in the gossip columns. Despite his rakish reputation, Montague was a most sought after guest and for a good reason. He cut a dashing figure; tall, with a lithe, athletic frame, which was built to display the latest fashions. He was handsome, in a boyish way, and his face perpetually wore a smile, which oft bordered on mischievous.

"I find I have no desire to gad about town this evening, my good fellow," Montague said, giving a sigh as long as a winter's night.

Jack frowned at this response; it was not like the Marquess of Thornbrook—who was heir to the Ducal seat of Staffordshire—to be so morose.

"Is something troubling you, Montague?" Jack ventured as a footman materialised with a drink for him. Perhaps his father, the fearsome duke, had finally put his foot down and insisted that Montague marry.

"I am out of love's favour," Montague sighed again, as he sipped on his brandy.

"Rosaline?"

Miss Rosaline Bowers was a former actress who had transitioned to the rather more lucrative role of courtesan. The beautiful temptress was under the care of the elderly, but extremely wealthy, Earl of Snowdon, and despite Montague's many attempts to woo her away, she could not be cajoled.

"Rosaline?" Montague frowned, "Lud, no. She was just a young man's infatuation, a distraction from the slings and arrows of this outrageous life."

A footman interrupted Montague's self-pitying monologue to deliver a steak, cooked to perfection by one of the chefs who manned the club's kitchen around the clock. It was to Montague's credit that he acknowledged the rotten timing of his remark with a self-deprecating grin.

"Well, perhaps I do not suffer so outrageously," he offered, as he tucked into his steak with gusto, "Physically I want for nothing, but spiritually my soul longs for…"

Montague trailed off, his eyes once more far away. He looked so distracted that Jack momentarily worried his friend might choke on his mouthful of rump-steak and never get to finish his sentence.

"For..?" Jack prompted, ever impatient.

"Lady Julia Cavendish," Montague admitted, having the good grace to look sheepish at his admission.

Jack stifled a sigh of irritation; trust Montague to yet again fall in love with a woman he could not have. The Cavendish and Montague families had been sworn enemies for centuries; the long-held grudge between them was so old, that few could actually recall why it had started. Not only would Lady Julia have little interest in the son of her family's greatest nemesis, but Montague's own father would disinherit him if he thought that his son might even be contemplating crossing enemy lines.

"You're a complicated man," Jack commented, as he waved for another brandy.

"That's rather an understatement," Montague grinned, "Though I am nothing if not adept at turning a complicated situation into something beautiful."

This was true; Montague had the devil's own luck. He could talk himself out of any scrape, and charm his way into any woman's bed, and had done both more times than he could count.

Jack paused for a moment to think. In matters of love, Montague—who had spent years seducing the ladies of London—had far more experience than Jack—who instead had spent years on the continent in the company of hairy, smelly men. The marquess was the best person to advise Jack on how to proceed with his courtship of Miss Havisham, but pride—and the knowledge that Montague would never allow Jack forget that he had helped him—forbid him to ask for assistance aloud.

Instead, Jack decided that a little subterfuge was in order.

"And how exactly would one ingratiate oneself with a lady who has no interest in being wooed?" Jack queried, mildly.

"Oh, it's easy enough," Montague's mood had improved vastly, now that they had moved on to his favourite subject, "You just have to be persistent. Some women are more difficult than others, and these are the ones whom you have to grow on."

"Grow on?" Jack raised an eyebrow.

"Yes," Montague grinned, "Like mould. Any housekeeper worth her salt will tell you that once mould sets in, it's impossible to be rid of."

"That doesn't sound very romantic," Jack frowned again.

"This isn't romance," Montague shrugged, "It's war. And in the end, you either win, sweet victory, or you—"

"Die a painful death?" Jack suggested.

"I was going to say you end up with bruised pride and a hangover," the marquess smiled, "But I have had many a hangover that felt like death. Did I ever tell you about the night in Carlton House, when Prinny got so sozzled, he rode a piebald pony down the staircase?"

Montague launched into a tale of his night with the Prince Regent, but Jack was only half listening. His friend's advice might not be very palatable, but given his success with women, Jack could not disregard it.

He must treat his courtship of Miss Havisham like a battle, Jack decided. He must plan a strategy. Mount an offence. He must...

Bring in reinforcements.

Jack bit back a groan, as the realisation that he had one great ally he could call upon to help him achieve his task—his sister.

5 CHAPTER FIVE

Even a day later, Violet still could not believe that she had managed to pull off her audacious scheme. While Sebastian's love for the theatre was what had landed her in hot water, it had also offered a way out. In her brother's cupboard, amongst the many costumes he had collected over the years, Violet had discovered a wig and a false beard. She had used a smear of spirit-gum to affix the beard to her face, and its effect had been alarmingly realistic.

She had then padded out the shoulders of one of Sebastian's coats with buckram wadding and donned a pair of his breeches, and when coupled with her height—which was above average for a woman—she had been unrecognisable as a woman.

Before the duke called, Violet had made certain to blow out a few candles in the sconces, to better aid her disguise, and she had practised affecting a low, masculine voice. True, it had sounded somewhat like she was suffering from a cold, but it had worked.

Violet shook her head again in disbelief, as her mind wandered over the events of the previous night. For the most part, she had remained in character, but she found she was still irritated by the one or two slips that she had made.

Men don't offer each other tea, she reminded herself sternly the next morning, as her carriage travelled the short distance from Jermyn Street toward St James' Square. And they certainly don't giggle girlishly when a duke declares his interest in their sister.

Violet's cheeks flushed at that particular memory. No man had ever taken an interest in her, and after three seasons she had almost believed herself invisible to the male of the species. To find out that a duke, of all people, had decided to take a fancy to her, was near unbelievable.

And utterly impractical, Violet reminded herself. No matter how taken she was by Orsino's green eyes—which were delightful— she could not encourage him to pursue her. Firstly, her scheme to take her brother's place until Orsino was finished with him would fall apart, for he would quickly realise the truth. And secondly, Violet sighed, romance was not in her own grand plan.

She wanted to paint. She wanted to travel. She wanted to learn from the great masters in Venice and Florence.

And none of that would be possible if she were to give in to the strange longing which Orsino inspired inside of her.

Besides, she frowned, the man had only declared that he had found her "interesting". That was hardly a proposal of marriage. And certainly not enough to inspire her to cast aside her lifelong dream.

The carriage soon drew up outside the home of Lord and Lady Cavendish, and Violet alighted without needing assistance. Which was lucky, for no assistance was forthcoming, given that it took Henry, the ancient driver, some ten minutes to get down from his perch.

"I shall be but a short while," Violet called to the octogenarian, who had refused all of Aunt Phoebe's offers to be pensioned off.

"Take yer time, Miss Violet," Henry replied with a lazy wave, contentedly resting back in his perch.

Violet felt a little guilty for having dragged the elderly man out at all. Jermyn Street adjoined St James' Square, and she could have walked the distance in five minutes, but one did not walk anywhere in London.

Well, not during the hours of morning calls, when the chances of being sighted were far higher.

"Miss Havisham," the butler who opened the door of Cavendish House greeted Violet in his usual, perfunctory manner. "Lady Julia had instructed that you might call."

His words contained a thinly disguised hint of distaste, for the staff of Cavendish House were as snobbish as the Marquess and Marchioness of Pembrook themselves. That Lady Julia insisted her friends be given free rein to call as they please—without even having to present a calling card—was, in the butler's view at least, akin to blasphemy.

Violet ignored the man's manners and followed him down the hallway to the drawing-room, where Julia awaited.

"Gosh," Violet cried, once the butler had closed the door behind her, "You look beautiful, Julia. Well, even more so than usual."

Lady Julia was considered the most beautiful girl in all of London. Even after three seasons, hers was the face against which all new debutantes were compared, and usually found lacking.

Today, she was resplendent in a morning dress of rose-coloured levantine, which was high at the neck and trimmed with a wide bouillonné of Irish lace at its hem. Her hair had been arranged loosely into a twist, and a few stray golden tendrils framed her heart-shaped face.

Violet's heart ached a little, as it always did when she was confronted by Julia's beauty. What would it be like, she wondered momentarily, to be so perfectly formed?

This slight stab of longing quickly left, as Violet recalled just what such beauty brought; queues of suitors a mile long, who cared not a jot for Julia's keen mind, but only her face and the triumph of winning her hand.

During their three years of friendship, Julia had received dozens of proposals and had refused each and every one. Like Violet and Charlotte, she had no desire to marry, but unlike Charlotte and Violet, Julia's parents were determined to see her wed.

"Mama insisted on a new morning dress for today," Julia said with a sigh, as she plucked at her skirts with a nervous hand. "I am apt to think of them as mourning weeds, however, for I fear her interference in my wardrobe means that my intended husband will be calling."

"No," Violet gasped, feeling somewhat horrified at how quickly Julia's parents had moved. She had confessed before to Violet and Charlotte, at one of their weekly wallflower gatherings, that her parents had declared that this season would be her last as a spinster. Violet had not thought that they would source a match so quickly.

Though she reasoned, Julia's beauty was coupled with a vast dowry, so perhaps it was not that surprising at all.

"Oh," Julia gave a wan smiled, "Don't fret. If he turns out to have halitosis and three heads, I'm certain that they will allow me to refuse. I am more worried that he will be—"

"Yes?" Violet prompted.

"I'm worried that he will be acceptable," Julia gave a shrug of her shoulders, "For then, I won't have any reason to refuse him. I have always known that one day I would need to marry, and if I am presented with an affable fellow, with good humour and the means to support me, what good will come of refusing him?"

Her statement was most sensible, and despite being in possession of a slight stubborn streak, Violet knew that Julia was at heart, a very practical young woman. The world presented few opportunities for a woman to make her own way in the world. Unlike Violet—who had Sebastian's enduring support, or Charlotte—who was currently working on a plot to earn her freedom, Julia had no fall-back plan.

While her parents would never cast her out into the street, they would, Violet knew, find some way of hiding Julia from the world if she disappointed them.

"Mama has said that if I am not married by the end of the season, that I will have to earn my keep and act as a companion to Aunt Mildred," Julia said, confirming Violet's theory.

"I don't recall ever having met your Aunt Mildred," Violet replied, searching her memory but drawing a blank.

"Oh, she's a real diamond of the first water," Julia gave a dry laugh, "One of her tenants was tragically widowed and left near penniless. When the widow's son was caught stealing a pig, Aunt Mildred personally attended court to make sure the lad was transported to the penal colonies and sent the widow to the poorhouse."

"Lud," Violet gasped, "How on earth did you discover that?"

"Because the woman boasts of it, constantly," Julia gave a sigh, "She is a firm believer that the weakest go to the wall."

Despite the sun which poured through the long windows, Violet gave a little shiver of fear. Her friend was truly stuck between a rock and a hard place.

"Perhaps," Violet ventured, wishing to find a solution, "If you were to find a husband of your own before the season ends, it might not be so dreadful?"

"Why try?" Julia shrugged again, "My parents will have put time and effort into researching potential suitors and ensuring that they meet their exacting standards. I know you think them cold, Violet, but they just want to ensure that I will continue to live as comfortable a life as is possible. I am blessed if you think on it. Truly blessed."

Violet bit her lip; Julia's determination to see the best in her situation did not quite disguise the despondency which had affected her spirit. Still, ever the consummate host, she quickly turned the conversation back around to Violet.

"You said you had something you needed to discuss?" Julia asked brightly, referring to the note that Violet had sent earlier.

Oh dear, Violet frowned; she had wanted to confide in Julia about the mess she had entangled herself in, but she could not now burden her friend when she had her own worries to contend with. Nor could she confide in Charlotte, who was dealing with her own meddlesome duke.

"Er, yes," Violet forced a smile, "I was wondering if you—if you—"

Violet had never been particularly adept at lying, and she felt her face flush under Julia's confused stare.

"If you had finished reading Glenarvon?" Violet blurted, referring to the book that they had assigned for discussion at last week's meeting of the Wallflowers. Well, the book that Charlotte had assigned. The running theme of most meetings was that Julia and Violet never quite managed to get around to reading the prescribed text.

"No," Julia blinked in confusion, "Is that what you wished to discuss?"

"Oh, it's really very good," Violet fibbed, though she could see Julia's mind quickly switching from perplexity to suspicion.

Thankfully, the door to the drawing-room swung open, and Lady Cavendish came bustling in, mercifully interrupting Violet's attempts at deception.

"He's here," the marchioness cried with delight, her face falling slightly as she spotted Violet, perched upon the chaise, "Oh. Hello, Miss Havisham."

"Good morning, my lady," Violet replied in return, trying not to feel too insulted by the disappointment in her tone, "I was just leaving."

"Oh," Lady Cavendish perked up most notably, "What a pity."

Violet ignored Julia rolling her eyes behind her mother's back as she bid the pair goodbye. She made her own way down the hallway toward the front door, where the butler was only too keen to assist with her exit.

As Violet tripped down the front steps, she tried not to peer too keenly at the gentleman who was exiting the carriage that had drawn up alongside Henry.

He was tall, muscular, and—Violet gave a little gasp—devastatingly handsome. As he passed, he offered Violet a polite smile, and Violet's fear for her friend eased somewhat. A man who handed out friendly grins to strangers could not be so bad.

Henry had fallen asleep in his perch, and it took Violet a good five minutes to rouse him. Once awake, they set off, circling the square before setting off toward home.

"There you are, Violet," Aunt Phoebe cried, swinging the door open before Violet had even had a chance to knock, "I have been searching all over for you."

"I told you at breakfast that I would visit with Julia," Violet reminded her, with a wry smile. Aunt Phoebe was oft distracted by grand ideas and regularly forgot any conversation which was not stimulating enough to retain.

"Did you?" Lady Havisham frowned, "I must not have heard you. That reminds me! Where on earth is your brother? I feel I haven't seen him in an age."

"He called, just yesterday," Violet replied swiftly, "When you were out. Was there something you needed me for, Aunt Phoebe?"

Violet nodded at the letter which her aunt held in her hand, and luckily it served as a distraction from any more talk of Sebastian.

"Oh, yes," Phoebe beamed, "We have received an invitation to a small gathering with Lord and Lady Lloyd. Iris is a dear friend, and she invites the most interesting people to dine with her."

"Oh," Violet felt a surge of relief that it was not an invitation to another musicale. Why the mothers of society thought that forcing people to suffer through butchered performances of the greats would win their daughters a proposal was anyone's guess.

"She is last-minute, as always," Phoebe clucked disapprovingly, despite her own legendary impulsiveness, "So if there is any dress that wants washing, you must tell Dorothy at once."

"Are we to attend this evening?" Violet smothered a groan; she had been looking forward to an evening of painting.

"Yes," Phoebe sighed, "Iris is a dear, but she can be quite commanding. She's so like her father that way. And, I suppose, her brother. You were not at all taken by him at Almack's, were you dear?"

For a moment, Violet felt as though all the world was spinning, and she worried that she might faint. Aunt Phoebe couldn't mean..?

"Oh, Orsino just looks fearsome," Phoebe cried, mistaking Violet's pallor for fear, "He's like a puppy underneath, you mark my words. A quick pat on the head and he'll soon come to heel."

"I don't want to bring the duke to heel," Violet protested, "In fact, I don't think I wish to accompany you at all, Aunt Phoebe. I feel really quite ill."

Aunt Phoebe's wrinkled her—already wrinkled—brow thoughtfully, as she assessed her niece. Violet tried to muster the look of one who was gravely ill, but under her aunt's scrutiny, she found herself flushing.

"I'll have Dorothy prepare you a nostrum," Phoebe decided, with a glint in her eye, "That ought to perk you up before supper. Now, away with you, child. I can't suffer the complaints of the youth when my old bones are aching."

"I am sorry, Aunt Phoebe," Violet replied, suitably chastised until Dorothy appeared, moments later, clutching two battledores and a shuttlecock.

"Are you going out to play?" Violet queried, raising an eyebrow in disbelief.

"I'm going out to win," Lady Havisham grumbled mulishly, with a frown, "That little madam from next door bested me yesterday evening, and I need to beat her today so that I can regain my dignity. Come, Dorothy, we shall leave Violet to recuperate."

Violet felt a stab of affection as she watched her septuagenarian aunt march down the hallway toward the drawing-room, which led to the gardens. She could think of no other peer who would do battle with the neighbour's children for the title of Battledore and Shuttlecock champion. Or any other peer who would take it quite so seriously...

And Phoebe's mission seemed to have distracted her from having Dorothy prepare one of her unpalatable nostrums for Violet's supposed illness. Violet would far rather suffer the duke's company than try to ingest one of those vile concoctions.

Iris, Lady Lloyd had the same colouring as her brother. Her dark hair was complemented by piercing green eyes, but unlike her brother, she was diminutive in stature.

She was almost like a bird, Violet thought, as Lady Lloyd cocked her head curiously to the side, as Aunt Phoebe introduced her.

"Miss Havisham," Lady Lloyd smiled, her grin warm and infectious, "How kind you are to attend my little gathering."

Lady Lloyd waved a lazy hand around the entrance hall, which was filled with guests of all descriptions. Violet spotted a well known Whig, an opera singer, and several of society's more notable lords and ladies. Given the glamour of the other guests, Violet was glad that Dorothy had insisted on dressing her in one of her better evening gowns.

"How kind you are to invite me," Violet replied sincerely, for, even though she suspected Orsino's hand in her invitation, she was quite taken by his charming sister.

Violet moved on, to allow Lady Lloyd to greet her other guests. Aunt Phoebe had disappeared, no doubt to the card room and Violet was left to wander alone.

She smiled shyly at people she vaguely recognised but felt too timid to join any of the chattering groups. Not for the first time in her life, Violet wished that she was in possession of an easy manner, which would allow her to converse with complete strangers. Instead, she found her cheeks burning, as she imagined that the gathered guests were eyeing her with pity or ridicule.

Oh, if only Sebastian were here, or Charlotte and Julia. Violet always felt far more confident when she was part of a group, rather than a stray sheep apart from the flock.

And a stray sheep was more than just lonely, it was a target for wolves...

Violet gave a little shiver, as she felt someone's gaze upon her. She lifted her eyes and sighted the Duke of Orsino, towering head and shoulders above the other guests, his eyes fixed intently upon her.

His lips quirked in a smile, as their eyes met, a silent greeting which felt wickedly intimate. Again, Violet shivered, but this time from longing.

He was decidedly handsome, Violet thought with a pang. Not handsome in the way of the Romantics, who were all floppy hair, delicate features, and mournful eyes. Nor was he handsome in the way of the dandies, who were as shiny and polished as a new pair of boots. No, Orsino's beauty lay in his masculinity, which Violet guessed was difficult to tame. Even tonight, though he was dressed as elegantly as all the other men, there was a hint of wildness to him.

His dark hair curled over his collar, the cravat at his neck was loosened, just a tad, and his strong square jaw showed a slight shadow, even though he had probably shaved only hours before. His skin was tanned and glowed with health, and his form—Violet bit her lip—was pure muscle.

Yes, there was something dangerous in Orsino's beauty, in his sheer masculinity...

But then his eyes, Violet sighed, his eyes were soft, which negated any of the hardness which his form projected onto the world.

Like poor Bagpipes, Violet decided, thinking upon her poor, misunderstood cat. People were frightened of the ferocious feline, but underneath his scraggly mane and sharp claws, he was really a kitten who longed to curl up in her lap.

Stop that, her inner voice cautioned sternly. If there was one thing that Violet adored, it was a misunderstood soul, and if she started feeling any sort of empathy toward Orsino, her future—as well as Sebastian's—was doomed.

He's a duke, she reminded herself with a sniff, he's hardly suffering the same loneliness and despair as an orphaned street Arab.

During all her musings, Violet had failed to notice that the duke had begun to make his way toward her from the opposite side of the room. It was only when he was in front of her—towering so tall that he near blocked out the light—that Violet realised she was trapped.

"Miss Havisham," the duke gave a neat bow.

"Your Grace," Violet tried to avert her eyes from his intent gaze but found that she could not.

"I was hoping to catch a word with you," Orsino continued gruffly, the tips of his ears burning red.

Was he nervous? Violet was faintly fascinated that such a large, powerful man could feel any fear in front of her.

"Oh?" Violet queried politely, praying that he was not studying her too closely and finding similarities between her and her "brother".

"Yes," Orsino paused, his face now burning as brightly as her own, "I—ah— I wondered if you…if you…"

Violet waited patiently for him to finish his sentence, her heart near bursting with a strange need—the need to comfort. As someone who oft stumbled on her words, or became tongue-tied when nervous, she felt a tremendous amount of empathy for the duke. He might hold one of the grandest titles in the land, but it was clear he was not accustomed or easy with expressing his feelings.

"I wondered if you thought it might rain?" Orsino finished, rather flatly.

Surely he had not walked all this way to discuss the weather? Violet stifled a smile, as she recalled their first conversation at Almack's, in which she had instructed him on the art of small talk.

Despite her vague disappointment at the banality of his query, she did feel rather touched that he had listened to her instruction.

"I see you have been practising the art of small talk, your Grace," she commented, rather mischievously, and Orsino's face relaxed into a smile.

"Perhaps I need to practice a little bit more," he replied with a grin.

"You might branch out from the weather," Violet suggested, "Perhaps offer a titbit on your hobbies or interests."

A heavy silence fell between them, as Orsino narrowed his eyes thoughtfully at her words. Despite her earlier vow not to be affected by him, Violet found that she could not help but be. His presence was overwhelming, and she found it difficult to breathe.

"Right now, I have only one interest," Orsino replied, after a pause, his eyes dark with intention, "And that is you, Miss Havisham."

Drat.

Oh, why had Violet decided to tease him? She should have offered him a polite, but very cold shoulder instead of an opening for further conversation. Time seemed to have stopped completely, and Violet realised that the duke was awaiting a reply—or any reaction at all.

Thankfully, fate intervened, and the gong for supper sounded out, breaking the heady spell between them.

"Supper," Violet trilled, not even trying to disguise the relief she felt.

Orsino quirked an amused brow at her blatant cowardice, before offering her his arm.

"I don't expect you to announce that you feel the same way," he continued, in a low voice, as he led her toward the dining room, "I simply wished for you to know my interest, and my intent to pursue that interest."

Violet gulped, too startled by his frank admission—and her own reaction to it—to offer a reply. Orsino silently escorted her to her seat, his gloved hand taking hers momentarily before he released her.

"My thanks, your Grace," Violet whispered, as she gratefully sank into her chair. The duke nodded silently in reply, before disappearing to his own seat near the head of the table.

Violet's shoulders sagged with relief, as he departed. She was not cut out for either romance or subterfuge, she thought sadly. The first made her knees week and the second made her heart pound with nerves—or, perhaps, it was the other way around?

She did not have time to ponder her conundrum for long, for the other guests began to take their places, and she was forced into socialising. Mercifully, Lady Lloyd had placed her near the top of her end of the table, and Violet had little to do except smile and laugh as the marchioness regaled her guests with her many tales.

After the first course of onion soup, Violet stole a glance down the table, to where Orsino was seated, next to Lord Lloyd, who sat at the head of the table. The duke, unlike his sister, ate silently, listening rather than talking to those around him.

"Ah, His Grace is the strong and silent type," a voice observed.

"Oh, I was not looking at His Grace," Violet objected quickly, "I was—I was admiring the chandelier. Such excellent craftsmanship."

"Ah-ha," Maria Grazia, the famous opera singer who sat to Violet's right, gave a throaty laugh, "You English are so puritan. He is a good looking man; it is no shame to appreciate beauty."

"Oh, I—I—I," Violet stammered, "Truly, I was just admiring the chandelier."

Maria Grazia laughed again, her warm brown eyes eyeing Violet affectionately. She was a striking woman, with sallow skin, raven black hair, and deep brown eyes that reminded Violet of her morning cup of chocolate. "If you say so," she said, flashing Violet a smile, "Though I fear that looking at His Grace is as far as we mere mortals shall ever get. He is promised to another if the rumours I hear are true. And he is far too honourable to stray."

Judging from the irritated sigh which followed Miss Grazia's announcement,

Violet assumed that she had some interest of her own in the duke. Violet was no green girl; she knew that powerful men kept beautiful mistresses. Though Maria Grazia's interest in the duke was not the only thing that had caught her attention.

"I had not heard that His Grace was engaged," Violet said, feigning nonchalance, though inside her mind was racing.

"Not officially," the opera singer dropped her voice to a low whisper and leaned closer to Violet, "But a little bird tells me that His Grace did the honourable thing after his brother's death and offered for the late duke's fiancée."

Lud. For the first time in her life, Violet wished that she kept up with the ton's gossiping. She wracked her brains to try and recall just who it was Orsino might have proposed to but found her mind was blank.

"Lady Olivia Cardigan," Miss Grazia helpfully supplied, perhaps sensing Violet's ignorance, "She was engaged to the late duke—a love match, no less. Rumour is that Orsino proposed the moment he assumed the title, but Lady Olivia has not been in a hurry to wed, given the recent loss of her brother. Whatever her reason for dallying, Orsino is not allowing himself to be caught in anyone else's net."

Maria Grazia gave a pout, leaving Violet to wonder if the alluring artist had attempted to snare the duke in her net. The opera singer turned away from Violet to converse with the gentleman beside her, leaving Violet to mull things over.

Orsino had proposed marriage to another; despite her vow to not be affected by the duke, Violet was astonished to discover that she was tremendously disappointed. Her heart, the treacherous thing, was sore and wounded. She had thought Orsino misunderstood and shy, but he was just another rake.

The supper was endless; eight elaborate courses, prepared by a French chef, followed by a selection of sweetmeats, cheeses, and wine. It was a sumptuous feast, though every mouthful tasted like chalk to Violet, whose stomach churned with anxiety.

Once the supper came to an end, the men retreated to the library to smoke cheroots and imbibe brandy, whilst the ladies repaired to the drawing-room for tea. Violet sat bolt upright on the chaise, beside Aunt Phoebe, willing time to pass so they could return home.

"What ails you, child?" Aunt Phoebe queried, prodding her gently with a bony finger.

"I do not feel well, aunt," Violet replied, and, unlike earlier, Lady Havisham appeared concerned.

"We shall away," Phoebe said decisively, rising to a stand with the assistance of her cane.

"Aunt Phoebe, it is far too early," Violet hissed, but the baroness paid no heed.

"When you reach my age, dear," she replied, without lowering her voice, "You may do as you wish. People don't tend to upset the elderly in case it finishes them off, and they come back to haunt them in revenge. I-RIS!"

Violet winced as Aunt Phoebe bellowed at their hostess. Lady Lloyd, to her credit, did not even raise an eyebrow. Instead, she crossed the room with a serene smile to see what Phoebe wanted.

"Thank you for a lovely supper, dear," Aunt Phoebe said, "But I must take my leave. These old bones need their rest."

"Pah," Lady Lloyd waved her excuse away with an airy hand, "If you of all people are leaving early, it means that I have failed in my mission to entertain. I will not listen to any excuses about age. Tell me, are you so bored, my lady, that you feel you must flee?"

"Oh, no," Violet interjected, not wishing to hurt Lady Lloyd's feelings, "It is I who am forcing her to leave early; I am not feeling well."

"Not the food, I hope?"

For a moment, Lady Iris did look genuinely nervous; nobody wished to be the hostess who left their guests running for the water-closet.

"A headache," Violet quickly fibbed, though it was not a lie, as such, for her head had begun to throb, "Perhaps from the excitement of it all."

"You do look pale, dear."

To Violet's surprise, Lady Lloyd reached out and took her hand, giving it a maternal squeeze. Her green eyes—rimmed with dark lashes, like her brother's—were kind, as she smiled at Violet.

"I can't deny that I am upset at not having had a chance to talk more," she said, "But now we have an excuse to meet again. The theatre, perhaps; Orsino rents one of the best boxes in Drury Lane. I shall write to let you know when."

Violet muttered a quick thanks, hoping against hope that no invitation would be forthcoming. She had no desire to be trapped in a small box with that great dolt of a duke.

Aunt Phoebe led the way from the drawing-room to the entrance hall, where the butler fetched their cloaks and called for their carriage. Violet's hopes that she might escape without having any further encounter with the duke were dashed when a familiar voice called out her name.

"Miss Havisham."

Orsino appeared, concern etched across his handsome face. Beside her, Violet felt Aunt Phoebe bristle.

"My niece is not the only lady present," Aunt Phoebe huffed, brandishing her cane in an alarming manner. Violet felt a stab of affection toward her aunt who, unknowingly, had lifted Violet's spirits. If only she had a cane of her own to brandish, she thought longingly.

"Excuse me, Lady Havisham," Orsino gave a neat bow in her direction, before returning his gaze to Violet. "I heard you were unwell."

"Yes, your Grace," Violet snipped, ignoring his confusion at her abruptness, "I shall return home."

"Ah," Orsino was obviously wrong-footed by her change of humour, "Might I be of assistance?"

"My aunt has called for our carriage," Violet shrugged, "Though thank you for your offer, your Grace."

Violet was not sure if it was bull-headedness or misplaced arrogance which caused Orsino to ignore her obvious coolness to him, for he persevered against her best efforts at subtle rudeness.

"I am sorry that you are leaving so soon," he said, his gaze sincere, "With your permission, I might call on you soon, to ensure that you are well."

Pah! Violet longed to poke her tongue out at the duke, who had the temerity to ask to call on her when he was promised to another.

Aunt Phoebe had also taken umbrage with the duke's request, for she cleared her throat irritably, and cast him a scowl.

"'Tis I you need to ask permission of, Orsino," Lady Havisham said, in her thick Scottish burr. Despite her diminutive stature, Aunt Phoebe could be quite terrifying. Violet was almost certain that Orsino paled, as Lady Havisham cast him a coolly appraising glance, her blue eyes traversing him from top to toe like a prize-fighter.

"You may call," Lady Havisham decided, having evidently decided that if it came to fisticuffs, she would win. "Then it's up to Violet to decide if she is at home when you do. Good evening, your Grace, our carriage has arrived."

Aunt Phoebe took Violet's arm and steered her toward the door and their means of escape. Violet made a pointed effort not to look over her shoulder as she left, though she could feel the eyes of the duke on her like a flame.

Her momentary happiness at having witnessed Aunt Phoebe put Orsino in his place, soon vanished as their carriage began the journey back to Jermyn Street. Although she had vowed not to encourage the duke in his apparent affections toward her, it still hurt to know that his affections had not been honourable—not even close.

Love is a smoke made with the fume of sighs, Violet thought darkly. She had never been a great admirer of the Bard, but having now experienced the pain of being disappointed in love, she could understand better why so many of his works ended in bloodshed.

6 CHAPTER SIX

While Jack knew that he had little experience with the ways of women, even he had the nous to realise that something was amiss with Miss Havisham.

On the first day that he had called on her, and she was not at home, he chalked it up to bad timing. When on the second day he presented his card, only to find that Miss Havisham was again "out", he decided that it was sheer bad luck.

On the third day, however, when the wizened gentleman who opened the door told him that Violet was not at home, Jack began to think that, perhaps, something had happened.

"Is she always this elusive?" he queried of the butler—who was so old that surely he was decades late for his appointment with St Peter.

"No," the butler answered, scratching his head thoughtfully, "And she never usually instructs me to tell people she's not at home, for no one really calls except her two friends of a Wednesday."

A-ha. Jack felt a moment of triumph, as he realised that he had been correct in assuming that Miss Havisham was avoiding him, which was swiftly followed by a feeling of gloom. What on earth had he done to earn her ire?

As Jack made his way back to his carriage, he cast his mind back to his evening at Iris' supper. In his eyes, the tête-à-tête that he had enjoyed with Violet—in which he had managed to remove his foot from his mouth long enough to profess his interest—had been the highlight of his romantic career thus far.

Miss Havisham too seemed to have reciprocated some of his desire. Jack was not so blind that he had missed her blushing—and it had entranced him completely. Nor had he missed her slight breathlessness and heaving bosom—though, of course, as a gentleman, he had categorically not been sneaking a glance at her bosom.

Everything had gone swimmingly; he had escorted her to supper—relishing the feeling of having her clutch his arm—and had deposited her at her seat. Her seat beside…

Lud. Jack groaned with annoyance; Violet had been seated beside Maria Grazia.

At the beginning of the season, the opera singer had made clear—on several occasions—her interest in becoming Jack's mistress. Maria had assumed that she was vying for a vacant position, when, in fact, she had been vying for a position which had never existed.

Jack had no mistress. Most aristocratic men did, well the ones with the means to provide for one did, at least, but not Jack.

He had gently—but firmly—informed the beautiful singer that he was not interested, but perhaps she had let slip to Violet her plans for him.

Though, Jack frowned, that was hardly the type of thing one would reveal to a stranger at a civilised supper. His mind wandered, as the carriage trundled from Jermyn Street toward St James' Square—a ridiculously short journey, but the nature of social calls necessitated a carriage. Jack cast his mind back over his few conversations with Miss Grazia until he recalled his last meeting with her.

"No," Jack groaned, dropping his head into his hands with despair. He had told Maria Grazia that he could not take her on as a mistress because he was promised to another—Lady Olivia. The love-life of a duke, especially one sitting at the same table, would, of course, be gossiped about by the guests. Jack groaned again; he had only used Lady Olivia's flimsy promise to consider his proposal as an excuse, though perhaps he had garnished the truth a little to dissuade Maria Grazia from her mission.

Well, perhaps he had garnished it a lot.

Oh, what a tangled web he had woven, Orsino thought darkly, as his carriage drew up outside Glamorgan House. His attempts at using Lady Olivia as a shield against Miss Grazia had inadvertently scuppered his fledgling romance with Miss Havisham. No wonder the poor girl had refused to see him—she probably thought him a rake of the highest order. And worse, there was no way in which Jack might be able to explain himself—at least not without exacting Lady Havisham's ire. One did not speak of faux engagements or would-be mistresses to young ladies unless one was willing to risk a box. And Jack had no doubt that Lady Havisham would deliver him a black eye more surely than Gentleman Jackson himself, if she thought that he had upset her niece.

Jack needed to explain himself and swiftly, but how…

Of course, Jack grinned, he could explain himself most plainly to Sebastian Havisham, who could then inform his sister—with a much-redacted version of events—that Jack was innocent.

"Grahams," Jack addressed the young footman who had opened the front door, "I shall need you to deliver a note to Jermyn Street post haste."

"Yes, your Grace," Grahams stood swiftly to attention and extended his hand for the letter which was not yet written.

"At ease," Jack instructed him, "I am yet to write my missive. Come to the library in a quarter of an hour, and it shall be ready then."

With a nod to his eager servant, Jack departed for the library, frantically wracking his brain for a valid excuse for calling on Havisham.

Later that night, just after ten bells, Jack knocked on the door of Havisham House. No light shone from any of the windows which faced out onto the street, and as he waited, Jack nervously wondered if, perhaps, no one was at home.

The muffled sound of footsteps approaching soon put paid to this thought, and after much clanking of bolts and locks, the door opened.

"Havisham," Jack said by way of greeting to Sebastian, who stood in the darkened hallway.

"Your Grace," he replied, his tone sounding rather surly to Jack's ear, "Won't you come in?"

Jack ignored his testy host and sauntered into the entrance hall. As before, the candles burned low in their sconces, offering little light and casting deep shadows.

"Thank you for agreeing to see me," Jack continued, as he followed Havisham down the hallway toward the library, "Especially at such short notice."

"Your note did not give the impression that my agreement was optional," Sebastian replied dryly, as he ushered Jack into the chaotic room.

Jack winced; perhaps he had laid it on a bit thick in his letter. His style of correspondence was perfunctory in a military way. Iris often said that she was never quite certain if she was being ordered somewhere, or invited when he wrote.

"I hope I have not interrupted your plans for the evening," Jack replied, by way of apology, "However, this is rather urgent."

Jack reached into the breast-pocket of his coat and fished out the "urgent" missive, which needed translation. The letter was, in fact, a year old, and had already been translated, but Havisham needn't know that.

Jack handed the folded page across to the young lad, who squinted at it for a moment.

"Shouldn't take long," Havisham muttered, before adding as an aside, "Would you care for a drink?"

Jack gave a nod, and Havisham retrieved two bottles from the cupboard. He poured Jack a healthy measure of cognac, before pouring himself a glass from the other bottle.

"Elderflower wine," Havisham said defensively, as he caught Jack's curious gaze, "I find it sits better with in my stomach."

Jack bit his lip to keep from smiling; Havisham was a slip of a man and evidently could not handle spirits as well as larger gentlemen. Jack himself, owing to his size, could drink brandy like water and never feel its effects.

"A man must know his limits," Jack said agreeably, as he reached for his own drink.

This seemed to settle Havisham, who sat down to work. The sound of his quill scratching against the page, as he wrote out the translation, was the only sound in the room for several minutes, as Jack waited for a suitable opportunity to bring up Violet.

"This is rather nice," Havisham said with some surprise, a while later, as he finished his glass of wine, "It does not taste at all like alcohol."

"Have another," Jack suggested, hoping that the drink might lubricate the young man's lips, for it already appeared to have lightened his mood.

Havisham cheerfully poured himself a second glass of wine and took a large sip. Jack waited a little while longer, until the second glass was near finished, before broaching the subject of Violet.

"How is your sister?" he queried, his attempt at sounding casual falling flat, as his deep voice cracked across the silence of the room.

"Eh?" Havisham glanced up from his work, the cheeks beneath his beard rosy-red—though from alcohol or indignation, Jack could not tell.

"I asked," Jack repeated, attempting to keep his voice calm, as frustration overwhelmed him, "After your sister."

From the irritated scowl that Havisham cast him, Jack knew that Violet had confided about him to her brother.

"She is well, thank you for asking."

A curt reply, which left no opening for further enquiries, was exactly what a man who wished to protect his sister from a rake should offer. Jack was torn between begrudging respect for Sebastian's loyalty and sheer frustration at his own predicament.

Thankfully, the army had trained him to master his impulses, and he valiantly ignored the urge to take Havisham by the shoulders and shake him until he offered news on Violet. Instead, Jack cleared his throat in a manner which let the lad know their conversation had not ended, before he spoke again.

"I called on her thrice," he said, keeping his eyes fixed on Havisham, who was staring pointedly at the page before him, "But she was not at home to me. Why do you think that is?"

The wine had obviously taken effect, for Havisham gave a derisive snort— the type one most definitely did not offer to a duke—and cast Jack a surly glare.

"Hmm," the lad said, stroking his beard as he faux-pondered Jack's question, "What on earth could have inspired my sister to refuse the calls of a duke? Could it, perhaps, be the fact that he is promised to another? Is that a reasonable enough excuse for His Grace, or is he so pig-headed that he thinks I—I—my sister should be grateful that he deigns to pay her any attention at all?"

Well. Jack exhaled slowly as he attempted to come to terms with the depth of Havisham's grievance. He could not blame the lad for being angry; had Iris been in a similar position, Jack was certain that he would be similarly apoplectic with rage. In fact, he rather admired Havisham for not having punched him in the face—with a brick—upon greeting him.

"I can explain," Jack began, leaning forward in his chair, "I know that Miss Havisham must be rather confused—"

"Not confused," Havisham corrected him, "Insulted."

"I did not mean to insult her," Jack growled, "In fact, I have not insulted her. I am not promised to anyone. When I assumed the title, I did the honourable thing and offered to marry Lady Olivia in my brother's place. She refused, but her father begged me to wait a while to see if she would change her mind."

"Well, the ton seems to think you in love with her," Havisham grumbled, "And why on earth would you remain semi-promised to a woman who does not wish to marry you?"

"Convenience," Jack was slightly shame-faced as he offered his answer, "It suits me to be thought of as off the market. I have no time for lovers or mistresses, and the only excuse for refusal most women seem to accept, without taking insult, is the love of another."

Havisham's face was now so red that Jack could have warmed his hands on it. For a young-blood, he seemed awfully prudish when it came to talk of mistresses.

"I did not think you a Puritan," Jack said with a laugh, "I'm sure you have half the demi-monde vying for a place under your bedsheets."

"Oh, no," Havisham squawked indignantly, "I have not—I have never—I am a virg—ooh, no..."

Havisham trailed off, nervously wiping his brow with the back of his hand, as he realised he had spoken too much.

Jack blinked; was the lad confessing what he thought he was confessing? If so, it was rather refreshing to hear—especially to Jack—for most men did little except boast of their bedroom prowess and conquests.

"No need to look so embarrassed," Jack grunted, "Wenching is a choice made by men who give little thought to the consequences of their actions. I have no time for it myself."

"Your Grace?" Havisham blinked his big, purple orbs in confusion. Jack could not fault the lad his perplexion; the papers had linked his name with dozens of women since he had assumed the title, yet Jack had bedded not one. Jack, in fact, had never bedded any woman.

"When I was a lad," Jack began, marvelling at how the brandy and the shadowed room had led him to a mood of confession, "My father had little time for me. I was the spare heir, and he felt that his time was better spent on educating Frederick in his duties. I was cast aside, and not being a great student, I spent much of my time outside in the stables. There, I was taken under the wing of the head groomsman, Evans. Evans was a proud Welshman, who taught me that honour, responsibility, and duty were what made a boy a man. It is because of him that I joined the army, and it is because of him that I discovered what really matters in life..."

Jack trailed off, shocked to find there was a slight lump in his throat. His childhood had been filled with all the material things a child could want for, but one thing—love—had been sorely missing. His mother had expired from a child-bed fever soon after delivering Jack, and his father had cared only for Frederick, his heir and protégé. Iris and Jack had been left to fend for themselves, and while Iris had found solace in reading, Jack had looked elsewhere and found it in the tiny cottage that Evans and his wife, Mavis, had occupied with their daughter, Gwen.

There, he had witnessed what true family really was. He had seen how Evans doted on Gwen, how she was the centre of his world, and that everything the man did, he did for his daughter.

Jack had seen what a father could truly be, if he cared.

"I could not, in good conscience, father a child and have nothing to do with its life," Jack shrugged, embarrassed by the croak of emotion in his voice, "The world is cold and cruel, and I could not bring a child into it, lest I knew that I could provide it with a home filled with love. Nor could I bed a woman, lest I knew that I could provide her with a home, protection, and my heart."

There was a momentary silence, as Jack finished speaking, and for a moment, he regretted his speech. It was not fashionable to admit to wanting love; Havisham was probably doubled over with mirth at his confession.

"His Grace is a romantic," the lad eventually replied, and Jack looked up to find Sebastian looking misty-eyed as he clutched his glass of wine—which had been refilled during Jack's soliloquy.

"I suppose I am," Jack shrugged, his cheeks burning a little, "Though, I beg you, don't tell anyone. I have a reputation as a cold-hearted brute to uphold."

"Pah! Men," Havisham muttered, rolling his eyes with annoyance, "Why must they always pretend to have no feelings?"

"You tell me why we must," Jack retorted with a laugh, "Or are you excluding yourself from the male of the species now, Havisham?"

The poor lad must have been deeper into his cups than Jack had assumed, for he knocked over his glass of wine in his haste to reply.

"No, no, no," Sebastian cried, "I am most definitely of the male of the species. So—so—so—what you are saying, is that you are not promised to Lady Olivia?"

The sudden change of topic was so swift that Jack's head ached. In the convivial atmosphere, which had fallen between the two men, Jack had forgotten the original purpose of his visit.

"No," he said flatly, "And I would be much obliged if you could explain that to your sister."

"Perhaps you are giving up on her too soon?" Havisham barrelled on, as though Jack had not spoken at all, "A love note or a sonnet might turn her head."

"I do not wish to turn Lady Olivia's head," Jack growled, "I do not love her. I—"

Jack cut himself off before he could finish his sentence, aware that professing love for a woman to whom he had spoken twice to was faintly ridiculous. Although, while he did not know himself to be in love with Violet Havisham, he knew that he could fall in love with her—if she just let him.

It was an inexplicable thing; a primal awareness of her beauty, a poetic understanding of her soul, a feeling of longing each time she was near him. Jack had never been given over to great feelings about anything, so he could not ignore the current of emotions that Miss Havisham had awoken in him. Nor could he ignore the strange feeling that he might drown in them, should she refuse him.

"Will you please," Jack continued, "Explain to your sister the truth of my circumstances."

His voice must have sounded pained, for Havisham nodded quietly in agreement.

"Do you think, should I call on her tomorrow, that she will receive me?" Jack ventured, hoping that he might finally get to begin his courtship of Violet.

"Oh, no, not tomorrow," Havisham replied quickly, "She has tickets to Saville House."

Jack's face must have expressed his confusion, for Havisham gave a sigh, before explaining further.

"Tickets to see Miss Linwood's exhibition," he continued, "Violet has been waiting all season to go see her work."

Jack vaguely recalled having read something about Miss Linwood's exhibition in the papers, and he made polite noises of interest, though really his mind was elsewhere.

He might not be able to call on Miss Havisham the next day, but that did not mean he could not by "chance" bump into her elsewhere.

"Right you are," Jack said, jumping to his feet, "My thanks, Havisham, for your time."

Jack leaned over to pick up his hat, which he had rested upon the table, and when he straightened up, he spotted Havisham peering at him with a mixture of confusion and suspicion.

"Did you forget something, your Grace?" the young man queried dryly.

"Eh?" Jack blinked in reply.

"Your urgent missive, which could not wait another day to be translated."
Sebastian Havisham held up the letter which he had spent the last hour
translating and waved it in the air for Jack to see. Jack flushed a little, thankful
for the shadowy room, which would hide his blushes.
"Yes, of course," he blustered, puffing his chest out and bringing himself up
to his full height, in order to look impressive. "With all our talk, I had
forgotten this was not a social visit, Havisham. Ah-ha. I'll just take that…"
Jack reached out and took the letter from Havisham's hand, with a small nod
of thanks. The lad's eyes seemed rather knowing, and beneath his beard, a
smile was definitely playing on his lips. Jack, who was accustomed to being
in control of most situations, was annoyed to have been caught out in his lie.
"I'd best be off," he growled, attempting to sound as important as he could
muster, "This is headed straight for Whitehall, to be examined. My thanks,
on behalf of the Crown, for your good work, Havisham."
It was a rather pompous declaration, but Jack felt that the use of a little pomp
and ceremony was one of the privileges of being a duke. If only to help soothe
his battered ego.
Havisham, who quite obviously did not believe a word of it, merely offered
Jack a polite smile.
"Please, don't let me keep you," he said, as he walked Jack from the library,
back to the front door, "I would not like to get in the way of, ah, urgent
Crown business. Goodnight, your Grace."
"And to you," Jack responded, donning his hat as he exited the door.
While it was obvious that he had not managed to disguise the true purpose
of his visit, Jack found that he did not care. He felt so light, that he near
skipped down the steps of Havisham House to his waiting carriage, his heart
full of hope for the next day.

7 CHAPTER SEVEN

Violet stood silently in the hallway for a moment after closing the door on Orsino. She listened as his footsteps clattered down the steps, and waited until she heard his carriage pull away before she let out a groan of frustration. Drat that man, she thought, as she stalked down the hallway back toward the library, where a fire still danced in the grate. Drat him, drat his soulful green eyes, and drat his romantic nature.

Far from being the rake Violet had presumed him to be, Orsino had unveiled himself to be the noblest of gentlemen. Violet's cheeks flushed a little, as she recalled their conversation, and said a silent prayer of thanks that Orsino would never know it was she whom he had confessed to.

Except he would, Violet paused, if he continued on his determined quest for Violet's hand.

"Drat," Violet whispered again, reaching for the bottle of elderflower wine upon the table. She did not usually imbibe alcohol, but given her current predicament, she could not help but fill another glass for herself.

Violet plonked herself back down at the desk, silently mulling over the night's events.

It was clear, now, that Orsino had called on a false pretext. The letter she had transcribed into English had mentioned places in France where—even Violet knew—fighting had long since ceased. Her suspicions that Orsino had merely brought the letter as a ruse to gain an audience with "Sebastian", were then confirmed when the ruddy-great man had sought to leave without it.

Thanks from the Crown indeed, Violet thought irritably, as she sipped upon her cordial-like drink.

She was in trouble for two reasons, Violet thought, with a jolt of shock. The first was that Orsino seemed determined to have her, and the second—and more frightening—was that Violet herself wanted Orsino to get his way.

It was not just the duke's handsomeness which appealed to Violet, but his goodness. Despite his large, brutish form, Orsino was gentle as a kitten—it was irritably appealing.

Not only that, but when he had spoken of siring children, Violet had been overcome with a vision of the huge, bulky man cradling a small babe, and found that she had wanted to weep with longing.

What would it be like, she wondered, to allow Orsino into her life? She would be protected, there was no doubt about that, but she would also be cherished. Cosseted from any hardship by a wealthy duke with a physique so perfect that it might have been sculpted by one of the masters.

"Stop that," Violet hissed to herself, pushing away her now empty glass. She could not afford to dwell on the duke's attributes or allow herself to dwell on what her life with him might be like, for there was no future for them. There was no "them". They were two singular beings, one of whom was a peer of the realm, the other of whom was…a liar.

Violet hung her head in shame, as she recalled Orsino's cracking voice, as he had determinedly declared that he would never sire a child he could not raise and love. His emotion had stemmed—Violet knew—from being thought of as second best. A feeling which Violet could identify with all too well. "Sebastian" had inspired a confidence, which was not deserved, and Violet was now riddled with guilt.

Imagine how hurt the duke would be, Violet fretted, if he were to find out that she had deceived him. Not to mention humiliated, annoyed, and angry. He could, Violet gulped, become so enraged that he might report her antics to her father—which would lead to big trouble for both Violet and Sebastian. Orsino had to be pulled off the course he was so intent upon, but how?

Violet sipped thoughtfully on her wine, as she pondered just how she might distract the duke from his inexplicable infatuation with her. As she sat, staring vacantly into space, Bagpipes rose from his position in front of the fire, sprung to the window sill, and scratched impatiently to be let out.

"I see you, I see you," Violet called to the impatient cat, who was now mewling with annoyance, "But if I let you out, you shan't get back in until morning—do you hear me?"

Bagpipes did not deign to reply; he simply fixed Violet with an irritable, amber-eyed glare, and scratched again on the window.

"Out you go," Violet said with a sigh, as she lifted the sash-window for the cat to make his escape, "But behave, and don't bring back any little presents!" The breeze from outside ruffled the hair of Violet's wig as she stood by the window, watching as Bagpipes stalked into the shadows of the night. Despite her warnings, she knew that Bagpipes would return in the morning, carrying the carcass of a dead bird or mouse which he would drop at Violet's feet proudly.

Although it would be a horrid sight and a very unwanted gift, it was touching to think that Bagpipes thought of her whilst out on his nightly adventures.

Violet made to close the window, but as she reached to draw the sash back down, light from one of the houses on Brury Street—whose gardens backed on to those on Jermyn Street—caught Violet's eye.

Lady Olivia!

The poor lady who had unknowingly caused Violet such distress occupied a house with her parents on that very street! The fact that she was so close felt almost like a sign to Violet. She hurriedly closed the window and stepped back, her mind racing a mile a minute.

Orsino had agreed to wait for Lady Olivia to make her mind up about his proposal—as an honourable man, he would surely not renege on his offer should she decide that she did want to be his duchess. Perhaps, if Orsino was to make some kind of romantic overture, he might help his lady decide on his proposal.

But how on earth could she persuade Orsino to put on a show of romance for Lady Olivia, when he was hell-bent on wooing Violet?

Violet closed her eyes against the dreadful idea which had struck her—Orsino need not do anything if Violet did it on his behalf.

She was already pretending to be Sebastian, Violet reasoned, as she reached for her quill again, what harm could come of pretending to be a duke?

Violet's hand moved quickly across the page, as though willing itself to outrun her conscience, which was lagging behind but beginning to make noise.

It's for the best, Violet told herself, Orsino needs an honest woman to be his wife, not a woman who dresses up as a man. Once her letter was finished, Violet slammed down her quill and stood up from the desk, hoping to leave before she talked herself out of her hare-brained scheme.

She slipped from the library into the kitchens, where she quietly let herself out the garden door. From there, she stole out onto the night street through the side-gate, leaving it unlatched so she might make a quiet return.

Violet had never been abroad after dark in London, and as she trod along the footpath, she thought nervously of footpads and thieves. Luckily, given that the hour was not yet past eleven, lights still shone from the windows of most houses, and the only people who passed were those in carriages, off to some grand event.

Violet turned onto Brury Street, clutching the letter in her hand nervously. She had planned to deliver the letter from "Orsino" to Lady Olivia herself, but as she neared the front steps, she wondered how on earth would she manage that? She could not knock, for no sensible servant would answer the door to an unexpected caller after dark. Nor could she simply leave the letter outside, for anyone might find it.

No more elderflower wine for you, Violet told herself sternly, as she realised that her brilliant plan was not so brilliant. She paused to survey the magnificent house, which stood three stories high and briefly wondered if she could climb up to one of the open windows.

I will end up hanging from Tyburn's Tree if I attempt that, Violet thought ruefully, or in Bedlam. Though, she was beginning to think that the latter venue was exactly where she belonged.

Violet turned on her heel, determined to scurry back home when the sight of a familiar, ginger beast caught her eye and put a halt to her departure.

Bagpipes!

The insolent cat ignored Violet, prancing past her with his tail up. He leapt from the footpath onto the railings of Lady Olivia's home, then hopped from window sill to window sill, until he reached a balcony on the second floor. Violet heard him mewling and scratching, and not too long after, she heard the click of a door opening.

"There you are, you little beast," a soft, feminine voice called, "Where have you been all day, eh?"

Bagpipes, the treacherous fiend! Violet was torn between indignation that her beloved cat was spending his time between two homes, and excitement that the person speaking might be Lady Olivia.

She stepped backwards, hoping to catch a glance of the lady on the balcony, but lost her footing in Sebastian's unfamiliar boots.

"Who's there?"

Violet's hopes of going unnoticed were dashed, as a beautiful young woman peered over the balustrades down to the street below.

"Lady Olivia," Violet gushed, as she scrambled back up to her feet, "Forgive me, I did not mean to startle you."

"And yet you did," Lady Olivia replied, casting a cool glance down at Violet, "Who are you? Tell me now, or I shall call for the Bow Street Runners."

Lud. Violet paled as she imagined the scandal that would ensue if she were to be escorted—dressed as a man—from beneath Lady Olivia's window by the Runners. The relative anonymity she had enjoyed since arriving to London would disappear, replaced by notoriety no young lady would wish for.

"I am Sebastian Havisham, my lady," Violet called, unable to think of a faux-moniker in her panic, "I have come to deliver a message from the Duke of Orsino."

Violet could not be certain, but she could have sworn that Lady Olivia gave an irritable sigh at the mention of Orsino's name. Nevertheless, Violet was determined to continue, so she nervously opened the letter that she held in her hand, and began to read it aloud.

"My sweet lady," Violet began, trying to keep her voice as low and masculine as possible, "Know that I love you, with adorations and fertile tears. With groans that thunder love, with sighs of fire—"

Violet had just begun to warm up to her speech, some of which she had appropriated from Shakespeare himself, but Lady Olivia seemed unimpressed.

"Enough," she called dryly, raising one hand to silence Violet. Bagpipes, who remained tucked under her other arm, purred happily in agreement.

Traitor, Violet thought, sourly eyeing her cat.

"I do not wish to hear about how Orsino thunders and groans for me," Lady Olivia gave a shiver, "In fact, if you are acting as a messenger, you might please tell His Grace that I have made up my mind. I have no desire to marry him now and never will."

Lud, Violet gulped, her plan to woo Lady Olivia had gone horribly, terribly wrong.

"But, he loves you," Violet called, stepping out from the shadows to plead her case.

"He does not know me," Lady Olivia replied softly, as she gently stroked Bagpipes head, "He offered for me out of a sense of honour, not a sense of love. Tell me, how can Orsino love me?"

"How can he not?" Violet shrugged helplessly, "You are the epitome of grace and beauty, my lady."

"Pah," Lady Olivia was suitably unimpressed by talk of appearances.

"And—and," Violet grasped for something else to offer, "You are soft of soul. Look at that mangy cat in your arms. Who else could love one as he, except a lady of kindness?"

"Mr Fluffykins is not mangy," Lady Olivia replied defensively, though she seemed more interested now in what Violet had to say, "Go on."

"You are a lady who has lost not one love, but two," Violet continued, "The stars have shone darkly upon you, and yet still you glow with vitality and life. What man could not love you? What man would not seek your hand?"

To Violet's surprise, Lady Olivia gave a wistful sigh at his words. She let go of Bagpipes and leaned upon the balustrades of her balcony, gazing down at Violet with a soft expression.

"You are a man of sweet words, Sebastian Havisham," Lady Olivia said, after a pause. She then offered Violet a smile which, to her eyes at least, looked awfully like the lady was attempting at being beguiling.

"They are not my words," Violet hastened to explain herself, "But Orsino's."

"La! Does Orsino think me such a fool that I can not recognise Shakespeare when it is quoted to me?"

Violet was spared from having to think of an excuse for "Orsino's" lack of originality by Bagpipes, who had returned to earth and decided that he wished to be in Violet's arms.

"Mr Fluffykins does not usually like strangers," Lady Olivia called in surprise, as the beast of a cat snuggled into Violet's arms.

"I am not a stranger," Violet retorted, her patience with her cat—and Lady Olivia—now at an end, "This cat belongs to me, and his name is Bagpipes, not Mr Whatever-it-is-you-call-him. If you are quite certain that I cannot speak on behalf of Orsino, then I must take my leave, my lady."

"Oh, I am certain that I have no desire to hear anything else from the duke," Lady Olivia replied, standing to a height and smiling down at her messenger, "But should you care to bring me any more sweet whispers, you would be most welcome. Goodnight, Mr Havisham."

Lady Olivia retreated from the balcony, with a coy smile over her shoulder to "Mr Havisham". As the door of the balcony clicked shut behind her, Violet let out a low groan.

Lud; what on earth had she done? She had set out to woo Lady Olivia on Orsino's behalf but had succeeded only in pushing her away. Away into the arms of "Sebastian Havisham".

"Don't you start," Violet hissed to Bagpipes, who had begun to squirm in her arms, "You are coming home with me, and there will be no more nocturnal adventures for you."

Nor for me, Violet added silently to herself as she beat a quick path back to Havisham House. For her own nocturnal venture had ended in a farce.

The next morning, Violet awoke with a thumping headache and a heavy feeling of doom. What on earth had she been thinking, she wondered, as she bathed and dressed, before heading downstairs for a much-needed cup of chocolate.

Aunt Phoebe was at the breakfast table, drinking a fragrant tea and perusing the morning's papers when Violet entered.

"La! You look like Prinny after one of his parties at Carton House," Phoebe commented as Violet took a seat, "What on earth has you looking so ill, my dear?"

"I did not sleep much, Aunt," Violet replied, as she reached for a piece of dry toast.

"Try not to stay up painting so late," Phoebe sighed in return before she stood from the table to begin her day, "It plays havoc on the complexion, and in your case, it seems to have brought on a beard."

Aunt Phoebe reached out to stroke Violet's cheek, with a mischievous glint in her eye, before she left the room bellowing for Dorothy. Nervously, Violet reached up to feel her face and found a small piece of her fake beard still stuck in place.

She hastily yanked it off, wincing slightly as the spirit-gum took a little of her skin with it.

She would have to be more careful, she thought, as she concealed the hair-piece in the pockets of her skirts. Her predicament was already troubling enough; she did not need to add to it by appearing at breakfast like a lost animal from Polito's Menagerie.

Nor did she need to add to her troubles by dragging other people into her lies, she thought with a pang of guilt, as she recalled Lady Olivia's smile to

"Sebastian".

Determined to outrun her troubles, or at least to stop thinking of them for a while, Violet finished her breakfast and ran to find Henry to ask him to prepare for their trip.

Saville House was located in the bustling hub of Leicester Square, and Henry was forced to circle for quite some time until he found a spot where he might park the carriage. Violet, who was bursting to finally see Miss Linwood's exhibition, sprang from the carriage as soon as it stopped.

"I shan't be more than an hour, Henry," she called over her shoulder, as she raced to the steps of Saville House.

Inside, away from the hustle and bustle of London, Violet found a quiet and calm entrance hall, where a fusty gentleman checked her name against his list before he permit her to enter.

Violet hesitated slightly, before the heavy, mahogany door, which led to the gallery. She had waited for so long to see Miss Linwood's famed works that she was almost afraid to enter. When she finally pushed the door open, she found a long gallery filled with light. High windows ran the length of the room, bathing everything in soft, spring sunshine, and allowing the viewer to truly appreciate the displayed artworks.

Each piece was stitched, not painted, and Miss Linwood's talent was so great that it was rumoured the Tsar of Russia had once tried to purchase one of her works.

Violet gave a happy sigh as she walked the line of the gallery, marvelling at the intricate detail in each of the pictures. How Miss Linwood had managed to create shadow and light so perfectly with a needle was beyond Violet's understanding—but then, she had always been terrible at needlework.

She halted before a reworking of Carlo Dolci's Salvator Mundi, which, it was universally agreed, was the gem of the collection. Violet leaned forward to peer at the picture; the embroidered stitches were so fine that one needed to squint to be certain that it was not a pencil or paint which had created the image.

A little further down the gallery, toward the door, two gentlemen were considering portraits of Napoleon and Lady Jane Grey, which hung side by side.

"Pah," one of them exclaimed, in tones more suited to a tavern than a gallery, "I think her overrated."

"Indeed," his companion agreed belligerently, frowning at the frames, "All this fuss over simple needlework? My dear wife works away quietly on hers in the evenings, without expecting any more recognition than my approval. Here, take a look at this handkerchief she stitched for me, is it not fine?"

Violet closed her eyes against the view of the offending conversation, which was unfurling before her, but unfortunately, she could not close her ears to it.

"Wonderful work," she heard the first gentleman exclaim, "And what more should a woman want than for her husband to appreciate her endeavours? Exhibiting needlework. They'll be asking for us to look at their oil-paintings next!"

Mercifully, the two gentlemen decided to take their leave, so offended were they by Miss Linwood's works, but behind them, they had left an unpalatable taste in Violet's mouth. How very like men, she thought churlishly, as she stalked along the carpet which ran the length of the hall, to think a woman's art should be produced only for the pleasure of her husband.

Violet huffed with annoyance, startling an elderly lady and her maid, who were eyeing a worsted work of a Rubens painting.

"I do beg your pardon," Violet stammered, as she passed them. She slowed her pace, exhaled a deep breath, and tried to focus her attention back on the artworks before her.

Violet spent a pleasant half-hour examining Miss Linwood's works, noting how cleverly the needlewoman had stitched silk into the thread to add light to create perfect replications of famed paintings.

She had just come to the end of the exhibition when an irritated "harrumph" from behind her caused her to turn on her heel.

"Miss Havisham," the Duke of Orsino towered above her, his face a disapproving moue, "What on earth are you doing?"

Violet paused as she tried to ascertain what on earth it was that she had done to vex the duke—he looked positively terrifying. Was it possible that he had discovered her duplicity?

No, she reasoned with herself; if he had, he would surely not confront her in such a public venue.

"I am taking in Miss Linwood's works, your Grace," she finally offered, frowning in response to his green-eyed glare.

"And where is your maid?" Orsino queried imperiously, with a glance over Violet's shoulder, looking for a maid who was not there. Violet had no lady's maid; instead, she shared Dorothy with Aunt Phoebe.

"At home," Violet snipped in response. His proprietary tone was beginning to grate on her; who was he to think he had any business in what Violet did, or where she went?

"So you came here, to the middle of Leicester Square, alone?" Orsino asked, indignantly drawing himself up to his full height, which was not inconsiderable.

"Yes," Violet now matched the duke's glare with one of her own. He was not the only one who could make faces, she thought churlishly, as she knitted her brow into a frown which she hoped looked as fearsome as his. "I came alone, your Grace. It is hardly the Seven Dials; it is an art gallery."

"It. Is. Dangerous," Orsino replied, his thick eyebrows drawing together into a scowl.

"Dangerous?" Violet raised her brow and glanced pointedly around the sedate gallery, which was empty bar the elderly lady whom Violet had almost barrelled into earlier.

Catching her gaze, the woman offered Violet a charming smile and reached into her reticule.

"Boiled sweet, my dear?" she asked, sending the maid over at Violet's nod of thanks, with a paper-wrapped parcel of humbugs.

"Thank you," Violet said sweetly, as she took one and pointedly popped it into her mouth for the irritated duke's benefit.

"Dangerous?" she whispered again, but this time her voice faltered. Orsino's eyes had turned dark and were focused steadily on Violet's lips. The same lips she had so smugly opened just moments ago.

Her mouth went dry as she saw something flash across Orsino's face, something deliciously wicked and dark. Something which Violet also felt as a pleasurable lurch in the pit of her stomach.

He is the only thing dangerous here, Violet thought nervously, as a queer feeling of longing overtook her.

She sucked nervously on her boiled sweet, so distracted by desire that the ruddy thing somehow lodged itself in the back of her throat. She gave a frantic cough, and Orsino sprang into action, leaping forward to deliver a resounding clap between her shoulder blades which dislodged the sweet—and sent her stumbling across the carpet.

She staggered, but the duke moved quickly, catching her in strong arms before she tumbled to the floor.

"See," he whispered triumphantly, as he helped her right herself, "It is dangerous to go out alone."

Violet longed to contradict him, but his arms were still wrapped around her, and she found that she could not utter a word. Her every sense was heightened. Her skin burned where he touched her. Her heart hammered in her ears. And his overwhelmingly masculine scent—wood, tobacco, and something earthy—threatened to drown her.

For his part, the duke abruptly stilled, as though he had suddenly become affected by holding her in his arms. After a heady moment, Orsino cleared his throat, dropped his arms from around her, and took a measured step backwards.

"If you will allow me to accompany you to your carriage," he said, his voice sounding somewhat strangled, "That is if you thought to come by carriage?"

"Of course I came by carriage," Violet was glad that his words allowed her to feel irritated again, for she could not stand this strange, heady desire which coursed through her veins. It was far easier to feel vexed with Orsino than attracted to him, "I know all about the risks posed by footpads and other villains."

"Good," Orsino harrumphed again, as he began to steer Violet in the direction of the door, "Then I will be glad to escort you safely back to it."

Oh, for goodness' sake, Violet thought, as the high-handed duke led the way outside. Does he think me incapable of making it down a set of steps alone? Her irritation must have shown on her face, for as they reached the carriage, Orsino offered her an apologetic smile.

"Forgive me," he said gruffly, "I was not expecting to find you alone."

"Were you expecting to find me inside, your Grace?" Violet replied innocently, determined to have a little fun with the duke.

"I-ah-I was not," Orsino lied, the tips of his ears burning, "It was a complete surprise to find you there. Alone. But what a coincidence, that you happened to procure tickets for the same day as I."

Violet bit her lip to keep from laughing; the duke was not about to admit that he had wrestled her day's itinerary from her "brother" the night before.

"Are you as taken by Miss Linwood's works as I, your Grace?" Violet queried, quashing the urge to giggle.

"Completely," Orsino nodded, his green eyes catching hers momentarily, and leaving her breathless.

"Tell me, which one is your favourite?" Violet continued, determined to plough on with her fun, for the alternative was to become lost in the sea-green depths of Orsino's gaze.

"Oh, I could not pick merely one."

Violet recognised bluster when she heard it, and Orsino's cheeks had now gone as red as his ears.

"Oh, that's no fun, your Grace," Violet replied, thoroughly enjoying herself now, "You'll have to pick one. I'm simply dying to know which piece you favour the most."

"Oh, look!" Orsino let out an audible sigh of relief, "We've reached your carriage."

They had indeed reached Violet's carriage, where Henry awaited. The elderly gentleman made moves to get down from his perch, but Orsino waved him away with a careless hand.

"I shall help Miss Havisham in," he called, as he guided Violet with a firm hand around the corner and out of view.

"I hope you don't think me presumptuous," Orsino continued, with a smile, "But I fear we might have been waiting a while for your man to get down to assist you."

"Yes," Violet agreed solemnly, "And in the interim, you might then have been forced to offer me an answer."

"Is it so obvious that I do not know a thing about Miss Linwood?" Orsino queried, with a rueful laugh.

"Only a little," Violet shrugged, unable to stop herself from answering his infectious grin with one of her own.

"I know nothing of Miss Linwood," Orsino admitted, dropping his head as he spoke so that some of his wavy hair fell forward into his eyes, "And I knew that you would be here, which is why I am here. I rather fear that as you were not accepting my calls, a little ingenuity was required on my part."

"Oh," Violet flushed at having been called out on her avoidance of him.

"I can't say that I blame you," Orsino ploughed on, "But now that your brother has had the chance to explain matters, I hope that I might see a lot more of you, Miss Havisham."

This was the moment, Violet thought, the moment that she should tell the duke that, in no uncertain terms, she would not be seeing him again. It was the most opportune time Violet would ever have, and yet, as she gazed at the handsome man who towered above her, her resolve wavered, and she could not find her voice.

"I am not the only one who wishes to spend more time with you," Orsino continued, taking Violet's silence for acquiescence, "My sister is determined to get to know you better. I believe she has invited you and Lady Havisham to the theatre this evening. The three Theatre Royals are staging Shakespeare plays concurrently, and tonight Haymarket will be staging Twelfth Night."

"Oh," Violet replied stupidly in response, as she wondered what on earth had happened to all the words she once knew—Orsino's presence and command of the situation had left her stuttering out monosyllables.

"Splendid," Orsino grinned, reaching out a large gloved hand to open the carriage door, "Until this evening, Miss Havisham."

Violet allowed the duke to take her hand and assist her into the compartment. She was not so dazed that she did not recognise the frisson of tension which passed through her at his touch.

"Goodbye, your Grace," she managed to say before Orsino shut the carriage door.

As Henry manoeuvred the vehicle into the traffic of Leicester Square, Violet sat back against the carriage seat, once again cursing her stupidity.

The perfect opportunity to stop Orsino on his stupid crusade to court her had slipped through her fingers because…she had no wish to stop him.

Curses, Violet thought despondently, as she now realised she was fighting on two fronts; against Orsino and her own foolish heart.

The feeling of dismay that she had tried to outrun that morning now pressed doubly down upon her as she returned to Havisham House.

"Oh, there you are, Violet," Dorothy called, as Violet trudged into the drawing-room, "Her ladyship was wondering where you'd got to."

"I told Aunt Phoebe that I would be in Saville House all morning," Violet gave an irritable sigh.

"I don't doubt you did," Dorothy smiled, "Though I didn't know what to say to your caller."

What caller? Violet frowned; social calls were made to ladies of influence, and as Violet had none of that, she never received any.

"Who was it who called, Dorothy?" Violet queried.

"Dashed if I can recall her name," Dorothy replied, "But she did leave a card."

Violet departed the drawing-room for the entrance hall, with Dorothy on her heels. There, in the silver tray which was used to collect cards left by callers—and which was usually empty—Violet found a cream, heavily embossed card, which bore the name of Lady Olivia Cardigan.

"Oh, Lud," Violet whispered to herself, before turning to question Dorothy, "What did she say?"

"Oh, not much," the lady's maid frowned as she tried to recall, "Just that she was keen to make the acquaintance of Sebastian Havisham's sister."

Oh, no; Violet resisted the urge to cover her face with her hands and sob.

"Oh," Dorothy clicked her fingers as she recalled one last detail, "And she said that she wants her cat back. Whatever that means."

8 CHAPTER EIGHT

Any peer worth his salt rented a box in one of the Royal Theatres, and Jack was no exception. Well, in truth, it was Frederick—who had adored the theatre—who had initially leased the box, but Jack had kept it on when he assumed the title.

He did not much frequent the theatre; being so tall, he found the seats small and uncomfortable, and as he was a man of action, he detested sitting still for so long. Still, one needed to make some sacrifices when it came to courting a lady, and Jack did not so much mind the thought of being cooped up in a tiny box if it meant he was cooped up beside Violet.

"Lud, you're fidgeting," Iris commented, as their carriage made its way through Covent Garden toward Drury Lane.

"I am not," Jack objected, resting his hands—which he had been twisting nervously together—flat on his lap.

Despite having nearly a foot on Iris, his sister always managed to make him feel like a misbehaved school-boy. Had Jack the romantic nous to carry out his battle for Violet's heart alone, he would not have asked for Iris' help, for—just like Montague—Iris would never let him forget that it was she who had helped him.

"I do hope you name your first child after me," Iris said, proving Jack's point.

"What if it is a boy?" Jack wondered, before abruptly pulling himself up, "La! Iris, you cannot start naming our children, when Miss Havisham has shown no interest in me. She is only here because you invited her, not I."

"Hush," Iris waved an impatient hand, "She is a free agent, is she not? If she really had no wish to come tonight, she might have cried off with a headache and allowed Lady Havisham to come alone."

Jack paled; he had not thought of that. Iris, reading his mind in the way that only a sister could, gave a tinkle of laughter at his glum countenance.

"She will not cry off, Jack," his sister assured him, "Mark my words. I know that you will insist on comparing yourself to dear Frederick and thinking yourself lacking, but there are a million things to recommend you as a husband."

"Such as?" Jack queried, horrified to find that he needed some words of reassurance.

"Your obscene wealth, for one," Iris laughed, though she quickly stopped herself when she saw her brother's downcast expression. "You are a wonderful man, Jack; kind, patient, amusing. There are any number of platitudes I could offer you, and they would all be true."

"Thank you, Iris," Jack grinned, "I don't know why, but tonight I feel especially like a great, giant lummox."

"Oh, there's nothing wrong with being large, brother dear," Iris twinkled, "Most women prefer it. I wonder how we might highlight it to your advantage tonight? Perhaps I might bribe one of the ushers to start a brawl and have someone break a chair over your back. That ought to be impressive."

As ever, Jack was not quite certain if his sister was jesting or deadly serious.

"I would suggest that we pay a footpad to stage an attempt to kidnap Miss Havisham as she exits," Iris continued, deadpan, "But then I rather fear that Lady Havisham would beat you to the rescue with her trusty cane, and that would not be impressive, now, would it?"

"Er, no," Jack replied, hoping to end the conversation before Iris dreamed up another scheme that she might actually think to act upon, "Perhaps we might forgo any tricks tonight, Iris. I might try to impress Miss Havisham the old fashioned way."

"What a wonderful idea," Iris agreed, leaning across the carriage to pat her brother's hand, "Just be you, and you shall win her heart. Though try not to scowl at her, as you do everyone else."

"I do not scowl," Jack objected, scowling across at her before quickly re-affixing his expression.

The carriage then drew up outside the Haymarket, and there was no more time for talking. Orsino exited first when the footman opened the door, and he then helped Iris down.

A great crush of people thronged around the entrance, and despite Jack's earlier promise not to scowl, he adopted the mien of the Duke of Thunder, as he escorted Iris through the crowds. People shrank back, as he made his way toward the door, and Jack was not certain, but he could have sworn he heard a small child scream.

"Well," Iris said with a laugh as they entered the elegant foyer, "I can't say there are not some advantages to having the tallest man in England as one's brother. Oh, look, there they are!"

Iris let out a cry, as she spotted Violet and Lady Havisham, standing by the steps. Several heads turned to see what was going on, and once they sighted

Jack, a ripple of whispers filled the room.

Lud; Jack bit back a sigh, he had hoped that no one would spot him on his mission. He did not wish for the papers to be filled with gossip about the evening, both for Violet's sake, and his own.

Montague was bound to find the whole thing terribly amusing, and while Jack could usually withstand his friend's ribald humour, his courtship of Miss Havisham felt too fragile to discuss with anyone bar Iris. His need for her left him feeling vulnerable, something he was not used to at all.

"Lady Havisham, Miss Havisham," Jack gave a neat bow, as they reached the pair. "How lovely to see you both."

"Can you see Lady Havisham?" Iris interrupted, "All I can see is half a dead peacock."

"At least I have deigned to dress myself," Lady Havisham groused in return, from under her feathers, "You seem to have dressed for a Grecian wedding, Iris. I am not entirely sure if it's a nightrail or a bedsheet you have on."

"The style is called à la grecque, my lady," Iris replied blithely, as she linked arms with the irascible Scotswoman, "It was the height of fashion during the Byzantine era when you were a girl, was it not?"

Jack watched with a bewildered grin, as his sister pulled Lady Havisham toward the stairs, leaving him and Violet alone.

"You'll have to excuse my sister," he said quietly, as he offered Violet his arm.

"Only if you excuse my aunt," she replied, with a shy smile. She hesitated for a moment, before placing her small hand on his forearm, and when she did, Jack noted that she seemed as affected by their nearness as he.

A pained silence fell between them, as Jack led them up the staircase toward their box. He was no good at small talk, especially with women. In the army, conversations had tended toward banter and lewdness, and he could hardly recite a risqué limerick to break the silence.

"I like your—your," Jack began, then lost track of what he had been about to say when Violet turned her bewitching, purple gaze upon him.

"I like your...you," Jack finished stupidly, flushing at his lack of verbal dexterity. Shakespeare, he was not.

"Your Grace," Violet replied after a pause, and Jack flinched, for he recognised from her cautionary tone that she was about to impart bad news. Thankfully, his heart was spared immediate damage by Lady Havisham, who turned to call—or rather bellow—to the pair to keep up.

"This is our box," Iris added, as she led the way to their seats.

Jack had to admire his sister, as she subtly arranged things so that Violet was placed beside Jack, in the darker corner of the box.

"Do you enjoy the theatre, Miss Havisham?" Jack inquired, once they were finally settled into their seats.

"I do," Violet kept her face turned forward as she replied, as though afraid to look at him, "Though I do not attend many plays. My brother is the true drama lover of the family."

"Ah, Sebastian," Jack smiled, happy to have something in common they might discuss, "We are acquainted. I wonder if he is here tonight?"

Jack peered out into the theatre, scanning the facing boxes and stalls for any sight of young Mr Havisham, whilst beside him, Violet let out a little squeak of dismay.

"Is anything amiss?" Jack queried, turning toward her with worry.

"A spider," Violet mumbled, her face pale, "But it is gone. Tell me, your Grace, do you attend many plays?"

"Not as many as I would like," Jack conceded, with a regretful wave to his large form, "I find that I am not built for such small spaces."

Miss Havisham's eyes followed the wave of his hand, and she blushed a little as he caught her appraisal. He had not noted until he said it, but the box was so small that Jack and Violet were almost pressed up against each other in their chairs. His thigh grazed hers, accidentally, and he was gratified that Miss Havisham let out a sharp sigh, which gave voice to his own sudden discomfort.

"Oh, look," Violet said, breathing a sigh of relief, "They're dimming the lights."

Indeed, the gaslights of the theatre had begun to flicker, and the roar of the crowd died down to a gentle hum. On stage, the curtains rose, and Jack settled back into his seat, to enjoy the night's performance as best he could.

For a while, he managed to focus his attention on the opening act of Twelfth Night but found his attention wandering toward the lady beside him. For her part, Violet appeared rapt by the play; her face was turned toward the stage, and her posture was rigid and straight. It was only when Jack moved slightly, and Miss Havisham immediately jumped, did Jack realise that her nerves were as highly attuned to him, as he to her.

It was rather gratifying to realise that Miss Havisham was not as immune to him as she might think she was.

"Well, what do you think so far?" Jack queried, as the curtains fell for the intermission, "Can't say that I find the storyline very plausible."

"Oh, it's more plausible than you might think, your Grace," Violet replied with a slight laugh before Iris interrupted.

"Orsino, you might fetch some lemonade and leave us ladies to converse amongst ourselves," Iris said, with a wink to Violet, "I am simply dying to interrogate the lady who has managed to finally get you to stick your head above the parapet of love."

Orsino's blushes only went unnoticed because Miss Havisham had turned as red as a beacon. Not only did she look embarrassed, but she also seemed faintly terrified of Iris. And who could blame her; his sister was famed for pushing the bounds of propriety for her own amusement.

"There will be no interrogation of my guests," Jack cautioned, adopting his most ducal expression in the face of Iris' sisterly mischief.

"La! Fine, I shall not interrogate the girl," Iris pouted, "Instead I shall offer her some sisterly advice on how best to control the men-folk. Did you know, Miss Havisham, that it was your aunt who helped me to tame Giles when we were first wed? He was prone to gadding about town, like he was still a young blood, but Lady Havisham advised me to have the servants move all the furniture in his chambers when he was out too late at White's. If he was too deep in his cups when he arrived home, he could not find his bed. Such fun!"

Lady Havisham boomed with laughter at this anecdote, whilst Violet looked torn between amusement and horror.

Jack sighed; perhaps it would have been better for Iris to interrogate Violet rather than give her free rein to tell stories.

"Iris," Jack whispered as he prepared to leave, "If I might appeal to your better nature?"

"I don't have one," Iris winked, "Now hurry along with the lemonade or I might amuse Miss Havisham with tales of your misspent youth. What was it that you called the dolly you carried around when you were five?"

Argh. Jack resisted the urge to groan in despair; instead, he cast Iris a warning glare, before he made his way downstairs in search of refreshments.

No man had ever procured lemonade as quickly as Jack did that evening. He used all of his muscle and mass to push his way through the crowds to where liveried waiters were handing out glasses of the cloudy drink.

Thankful that his hands were large enough to easily manage four glasses, Jack raced back to the box, just in time to hear Iris finish detailing how she used to make Jack dress up in a gown for play tea-parties.

"You are determined to embarrass me, sister dearest," Jack said through gritted teeth, as he passed the glasses to each of the ladies.

"Not at all," Iris protested, "I was merely trying to paint an accurate picture of you for Miss Havisham. You present such a rugged, manly exterior to the world that it is difficult for people to believe that you have a softer side. He is incredibly soft-hearted, Miss Havisham."

"But I have not worn a dress in many years," Jack was quick to clarify, "And even then, it was under duress. Iris was quite the tyrannical older sister."

"Oh, I know something of domineering siblings," Miss Havisham gave a light laugh, "Sebastian once convinced me to cut off all my hair and go in his stead to Eton."

"Really?" Jack raised an eyebrow, "I cannot imagine you made a very convincing boy; your looks are far too feminine."

Violet made a strangled sound, halfway between a laugh and a cry. Jack blinked a little, unsure if this was the usual female response to compliments. Any further enquiries he might have wished to make were abandoned by the arrival of two guests, who poked their heads around the curtains of the box.

"Your Grace, Lady Iris," Lady Cardigan cried in greeting, "I thought that it was you whom I spotted."

It took Herculean effort for Jack not to curse aloud at the arrival of Lady Cardigan, a woman he usually had great time for. Beside her, still dressed in half-mourning, stood Lady Olivia, appearing as pained as Jack felt.

"Oh, you have guests," Lady Cardigan glanced pointedly at Violet and Lady Havisham, and Iris hastened to make an introduction.

"I have heard a great deal about you from your nephew, Lady Havisham," Lady Cardigan said congenially, before turning to Violet with a frown, "Though I was not aware that Waldo had a daughter; he has never mentioned you, my dear."

"That is no surprise," Violet whispered, so quietly that Jack assumed it had not been said to be heard. He frowned a little, as he watched Miss Havisham rearrange her fine features into a pleasant smile, as she listened to the three ladies chattering. Jack, who had spent his youth as an unneeded spare, recognised well the flash of pain that had dulled Violet's eyes. He understood all too well how it felt to never quite matter.

Lady Olivia stood slightly to the right of her mother, her blue eyes glazed with boredom. It was only when Lady Cardigan made noises about returning to their seats, that the young woman finally spoke.

"Is Mr Havisham with you?" she queried of Lady Havisham, whilst fidgeting nervously with a strand of her hair.

"Sebastian?" Lady Havisham boomed, "Chance would be a fine thing, I have not seen the lad in weeks. Violet, where has your brother got to?"

Jack watched as Violet paled and bit on her rosebud mouth nervously. He was so distracted by thoughts of himself nibbling on that lush bottom lip that he missed her response, and by the time his mind had righted itself, the gaslights were flickering for the second half of the play.

Jack allowed a few minutes to pass before he shifted in his seat slightly, to whisper in Violet's ear.

"I cannot believe that your father has never mentioned you to Lady Cardigan," he said in a low voice, "I am sure that he speaks highly of you to everyone he meets."

A very unladylike snort greeted this statement before Violet turned her face toward him to reply.

"I am afraid that you store far more faith in my father than I do," she said, as a sad smile played around the corners of her mouth, "He has room in his heart only for Sebastian."

"Then he is a fool," Jack growled, and to his—and Violet's—surprise, he reached out and took her hand in his.

He had meant to offer her a comforting squeeze, but as Jack held her small, gloved hand in his, he found that he could not simply squeeze it and let it go. So instead, he kept a hold of it for the remainder of the play.

The two final acts of the play passed in a blur, as Jack concentrated on savouring the feeling of Violet's hand in his. For her part, she did not tense, or try and snatch her hand away, and when the play finally came to an end, and the gas lights flickered back on, Jack was gratified to find that her cheeks were rosy, and she seemed as flustered as he.

"Well, that was simply wonderful," Iris cried, as their group began to find their feet.

"Indeed," Jack replied, hoping she would not question him on any aspect of the play, for he could not recall a second of it.

Iris and Lady Havisham led the way back downstairs, both debating the merits of the play and its actors.

"Were you taken with the performance, Miss Havisham?" Jack queried lightly as they neared the foyer.

"I can't say that I can recall much of it, your Grace," she replied, as her cheeks turned rosy red.

Within Jack's chest, male pride roared, and for the first time, he understood why Montague happily dove headfirst into love every few months—it was intoxicating.

When love speaks, the voice of all the gods makes heaven drowsy with the harmony. Orsino had not been the brightest of students, but as he led Violet through the crowded foyer, a quote from Shakespeare sprang to mind. He felt as light and fluffy as a cloud—something he seldom experienced, given that he was built as solid as a rock.

As they neared the doorway, where they would wait for their carriage, Jack felt an urgent need to secure a promise from Violet that they would meet again.

"I would like to call on you tomorrow," he said, nervously clearing his throat.

"Ah."

With one syllable, Jack felt his heart drop to his feet.

"I am afraid that tomorrow I have made plans," Violet offered, "With my friends Miss Charlotte Drew and Lady Julia. We meet once a week to discuss the prescribed text that Charlotte has set. Tomorrow we are discussing *Evelina*."

"Is it good?" Jack asked as hope fluttered anew. Surely she would not have offered so detailed an excuse if she was simply trying to fob him off.

"Heaven knows, your Grace," Violet laughed, "I have not read it. I am afraid that Miss Drew is the only one who ever reads the books she sets. Lady Julia and I are just there for the French Fancies."

Not for the first time in his life, Jack wondered at the complexities of the female species, who always seemed to think one needed an excuse to eat cake. Still, Violet had not dashed his hopes completely, and ever the soldier, he battled on.

"And the day after that?" he pressed, wondering if perhaps he might find a way to wiggle into one day of her schedule.

"A ball at Lord and Lady Jacob's."

"Ah, what a coincidence," Jack fibbed, "I had planned to attend that too. I hope that you will be kind enough to save me a dance, Miss Havisham."

"If there is one thing you do not have to worry about, your Grace," Violet laughed in reply, "It is finding me with a full dance card. You might have your pick of them if you wish."

"If that is the case," Jack lowered his voice to a soft growl, "Then I pick them all, Miss Havisham. All your dances."

If he were braver, Jack might have added that he wanted to claim all her dances forevermore, but he was still a little unsure of Miss Havisham. Oh, he was certain that she felt the same attraction to him, as he to her. But she was still reticent, still nervous of admitting it even to herself. Her brother's assertion that Miss Havisham was the most determined spinster still played in Jack's mind, and he was afraid that if he revealed the depth of his intentions too soon, she might flee like a skittish doe.

Any further conversation was prevented as the pair caught up with Iris and Lady Havisham, who were waiting for them at the door. Jack took charge and bid the doorman summon their carriages. Once they had arrived, he assisted first Lady Havisham, and then Violet, into their vehicle, before returning for Iris.

"Well," his sister said, once they were seated inside their compartment and headed for home, "That went very well."

"Do you think?" Jack questioned, hopefully. His sister was more attuned to the mysterious female nuances and signals, and if she believed Miss Havisham interested in him, then it had to be true.

"Oh, yes," Iris gave a cat-like smile, "It's clear as day that Lady Olivia is infatuated by Sebastian Havisham."

"Really?" Jack blinked; how on earth had she ascertained that?

"Yes," Iris nodded, "Which lets you off the hook on that front. And as for Miss Havisham."

"Yes?" Jack sat up straight, rapt with attention.

"I think it would be best if I bought a new hat."

Well, Jack thought, once he had deciphered her code, this did bode well.

9 CHAPTER NINE

Violet was not often given over to bouts of sorrow, or maudlin thoughts, but the following morning she found that she could not shake the grey cloud of despair which hung over her.

It had everything to do with the Duke of Orsino, she thought, as she dabbed her paintbrush against the canvas, and then, it had nothing to do with him at all.

She could not blame the duke for the hopeless mess that she had landed herself in; any criticism lay at her own foolish door. Nor could she blame him for her attraction toward him—though it was almost rude how handsome he was.

Rude, Violet decided, as she stabbed her paintbrush with more vigour than was necessary; it was rude to be so large and strong and masculine and think that it would go unnoticed in a confined space.

He should have—he should have—

Violet sighed as her efforts to find irritation with Orsino fell flat. Did she truly expect that he should have curled up into a ball and pretended not to be a strapping, six-foot-four duke simply to appease her? It might be painful, but she had to accept that any irritation she felt should be directed at herself and her own silly actions.

For a moment, Violet allowed herself to imagine a parallel world; a world where she had not thought that imitating her brother was a sane course of action. In that world, she imagined herself floating on air, having spent the previous evening having her hand held by a duke.

Sebastian had once entertained her with the tale of how Zeus, the first God and king of Mount Olympus, had split humans in two. This was, according to Sebastian, because humans were originally created with four arms, four legs and a head with two faces, and Zeus feared their power. While her brother had been boyishly entranced by the idea of such a monstrous four-legged creature, Violet had been struck dumb by his flippant finishing remark, that by splitting them in two, Zeus had thusly condemned humans to spend their lives in search of their other halves.

Last night, in the theatre, with the sting of Lady Cardigan's comment still burning Violet's heart, Orsino had reached out and taken her hand. He had, she knew, also felt the burning shame of being rejected by one's own father in favour of another. And he had recognised it within her and sought to make it better.

It was far-fetched and even fanciful, but at that moment, Violet had felt as though she had found her missing half.

Well, even if you have found him, you'll have to quickly lose him, a stern voice in her head cautioned, drawing an end to Violet's fantasy.

There was no way that Violet could ever find happiness with Orsino, not when she had deceived him so. She briefly flirted with the idea of revealing to the duke what she had done, but when she imagined his reaction—hurt, humiliation, anger—her bravery faltered. The thought that Orsino might be disappointed in her caused her anguish akin to a physical blow.

Though those that are betrayed do feel the treason sharply, yet the traitor stands in worse case of woe.

Thanks to Sebastian, Violet could quote reams of Shakespeare, and the line from Cymbeline felt particularly apt for her particular quandary.

There was nothing for it, she thought sadly, but to embrace her cursed fate and spend the rest of her life ruing her impulsiveness.

For the rest of the morning, Violet attempted to concentrate on her current work; a portrait of Aunt Phoebe, in the style of Marguerite Gérard. The French artist was famed for depicting intimate, domestic scenes, and Violet's own painting showed Phoebe, snoozing in her chair, with Fifi by her feet.

Though Violet thought wryly, Phoebe was asleep in the painting because that was the only way Violet could get her to sit long enough to be painted. Thank heavens Fifi was inanimate, or Violet might never finish her work.

At eleven o'clock, Violet removed her apron and began to clean down her brushes and pallet, in preparation for the arrival of her friends.

Charlotte was the first to arrive, a whirligig of energy and excitement, as she loudly proclaimed that she would broker discussion of nought but Evelina.

"It's an exploration of the complex layers of society," Charlotte stated primly, "It's wonderfully satirical, and it is said that it was a significant precursor to the works of Miss Austen and Miss Edgeworth—one of whom's books we shall be reading next week. What did you think of it, Violet?"

"Eh," Violet floundered for something to say, but thankfully Julia's arrival saved her.

"What did you think of Evelina, Julia?" Charlotte called to their friend by way of greeting.

"La! You shan't distract me with talk of books, Cat," Julia answered, treading her way carefully across the room to the chaise, "I want to know exactly what happened with you and Penrith at the theatre. The papers were full of speculation about you both—it seems your plan is working."

"Pfft," Charlotte exhaled impatiently, "I have no desire to discuss Penrith. None whatsoever."

"Well, if you'd rather discuss Evelina, I'm all ears," Julia replied, flashing Violet a wink.

There was a pause, as Charlotte visibly battled against her desire to finally discuss literature at one of their meetings, and her need to dissect her duke. Dissection won out.

"Well," Charlotte gave a frustrated sigh, before launching into a long tale of her excursion with Penrith the night before. There was much grumbling, heaps of expressed irritation, some self-righteousness, and an awful lot of emotion; but the sub-text was quite clear to both Violet and Julia, who watched their friend in amusement.

"He really is most infuriating," Charlotte finished with a sigh, as she placed her cup of tea down upon the table.

"Yes, you've said that three times already," Julia replied, attempting to hide a smile behind her own cup.

"Actually, it's four times by my count," Violet offered, unable to disguise her own amusement at Charlotte's outrage.

It was obvious to even a casual observer, that the Duke of Penrith had wiggled his way under Charlotte's skin, and was causing her all kinds of bother. As Violet knew Charlotte so well, she could tell that her friend was struggling with her feelings for the duke—who was the antithesis of the type of man that Charlotte, a rebellious libertarian, would fall for.

Charlotte would happily have fallen head over heels for an artist, a writer, or any other egalitarian sort, but here she was, clearly smitten with a Tory.

No wonder her head was stubbornly fighting against her heart; though Violet rather thought that her heart would win out.

Charlotte flustered and blustered for a moment, but perhaps fearing that she was unable to disguise her true feelings, turned the conversation toward Violet's painting.

"Why, Violet, it's genius," Charlotte pronounced, as she took in her friend's depiction of a domestic scene, "You're well on your way to becoming the next Marguerite Gérard."

Violet, who was not certain if Charlotte truly meant what she said, or only said it because she knew that Marguerite Gérard was her favourite artist, gave a helpless shrug.

"Marguerite Gérard had residence in the Louvre, and was surrounded by artists and great masterpieces," Violet grumbled in response, "I can never hope to emulate her when all I am surrounded by are piles of books and stuffed dogs."

Violet poked poor Fifi despondently with the end of her paintbrush. The rigid terrier toppled over onto her side, her glass eyes staring up sadly at the trio of young ladies.

"You are not only surrounded by dead dogs," Julia replied bracingly, "You have two friends who think you are a marvellous painter. And you have Sebastian, a true connoisseur of the arts. Where is he? Perhaps he can offer a word of encouragement?"

Lud! Violet jumped at the mention of Sebastian's name. She might be able to hide his absence from Aunt Phoebe, but she would never be able to fool Julia and Charlotte if they began to suspect something was amiss.

"S-S-Sebastian?" Violet stuttered, in response, desperate to move away from the topic of her twin, "Why should we need to call Sebastian? The two of you have supplied me with all the encouragement I need. Come, let us forget the painting for a moment and focus on the real issue at hand; Charlotte's love for Penrith."

It was a low-blow, outing Charlotte as a dukeophile in order to distract, but thankfully her friend leapt at the bait.

"I beg your pardon?" Charlotte squawked as Violet corralled her friends back to the table where the tea and cakes had been set out.

"It's quite obvious that you are infatuated by him," Violet replied, quashing some guilt, as she poured three fresh cups of tea, "You have talked of nothing else since you arrived."

"I have not!" Charlotte argued, taking the cup that Violet proffered.

"The lady doth protest too much, methinks," Julia said with a smile, as she settled herself back onto the sofa.

"If I was bleating about His Grace, it is only because I find him so annoying," Charlotte was quick to defend herself.

The conversation soon descended into a cheerful argument which pitted a stubborn Charlotte against Julia and Violet, who were keen to point out their friend's obvious infatuation.

"La! You are both incorrigible," Charlotte finished with a cry, as she gathered her bits together to prepare to leave, "And fit for Bedlam if you think that I am interested in Penrith for anything except my own liberation. Now, next week I should like us to discuss Castle Rackrent; Miss Edgeworth intended it as a satirical take on the upper classes, much like Evelina—which you would both know, had you bothered to read it. Good day, ladies."

Charlotte bustled from the room, with an air of self-righteousness, leaving an amused Julia and Violet alone.

"Well," Julia said lightly, once the door had closed behind their friend, "Now we have discussed Penrith to death, it's time to execute Orsino."

Violet, who had been munching on a French Fancy, began to choke at the mention of his name.

"Both Penrith and Charlotte command a greater degree of notoriety than you and Orsino," Julia continued, cool as a cucumber, "But don't think that I did not notice the small column which noted his attendance at the Haymarket, accompanied by none other than you, Miss Havisham."

"Did they mention me particularly?" Violet queried; she had never once been mentioned by the papers, a fact she owed to her lack of fortune. Charlotte, who had a dowry greater than the king's coffers, had long been a favourite of the gossip columns, even though she did not court their attention.

"Well, no," Julia shifted uncomfortably in her seat, "They did not name you per se—they said Lady Havisham and her niece."

"The world has not gone mad, so," Violet breathed a sigh of relief, "If I am still merely a nameless companion."

"To some you are nameless," Julia countered with a frown, "But I knew exactly whom they were speaking of. Tell me, why on earth did you not mention you accompanied Orsino to the theatre?"

"Because I did not," Violet lied, "I accompanied Aunt Phoebe, who was invited by Lady Lloyd, who was in turn, accompanied by her brother."

"So, your presence in the box with Orsino was merely coincidental?" Julia pressed.

"Yes," Violet pressed her lips together as she attempted to emulate Charlotte's famed stubbornness.

"So, you did not at all hold His Grace's hand?"

"Did the papers say that?" Violet gawped, "How on earth did they know?"

"They didn't," Julia grinned in triumph, "I made it up—but what a lucky guess! Violet, you are a dark horse. Why on earth did you keep Orsino's courtship a secret?"

"It's not a courtship," Violet, whose pride was slightly rankled at having been so easily tripped, replied, "His Grace invited me to the theatre, I attended; end of story. There is no happily ever after in store for the duke and me, Julia—you can take my word on that."

Violet knew that she had spoken far more forcefully and touchily than one should speak to a friend, and she instantly regretted her curt manner. Thankfully, Julia was the most unflappable sort of girl, and she did not immediately show any grievance. In fact, her beautiful face wore a look of concern.

"What is it, Vi?" Julia asked, leaning forward to place a slim, gloved hand upon Violet's own, "You have been out of sorts for weeks. It is not like you at all to be so jumpy and irritable. Is something troubling you? If there is, I beg you, please tell me."

Violet felt a fierce longing to unburden herself to her friend, but how on earth could she explain the madness she had landed herself in? For a moment, Violet considered telling Julia, but in the instant that she hesitated, a knock came upon the parlour-room door.

"Begging your pardon, m' lady," Maria, Julia's lady's maid, called, "But we'd best be away if we are to be on time to meet your mama."

"Lud," Julia was uncharacteristically sullen, "I had forgotten about the dress fitting. Mama will have an apoplectic fit if I am late—she had to use all her societal sway to secure an appointment with Madam Lloris so late in the season."

"Er, why exactly do you need a special dress made so late into the season?" Violet queried, her mind instantly leaping to one conclusion.

"For a masquerade," Julia gave a light laugh, as she noted Violet's suspicion, "Have no fear if I become engaged, I will let you know."

"Do you feel an engagement is an imminent possibility?" Violet pressed, wondering at Julia's cool composure. Any thoughts of Orsino left Violet feeling flustered, but here Julia was, cool as a cucumber as she discussed her possible future husband.

"Lord Pariseau is perfectly affable," Julia shrugged, her blue eyes dull, "And don't you look at me like that, Violet! I am not an artist; I have not a romantic bone in my body. Marriage, to me, is a practical arrangement—one which will ensure my future comfort and happiness. If you and Charlotte had your way, you'd have me married off to Lord Montague so we could all have an Upstart of our own."

"I don't recall anyone mentioning Lord Montague, Julia?" Violet replied, then watched in fascination, as her usually composed friend blushed—actually blushed.

"Well, it would be the sort of ridiculous thing the two of you would dream up," Julia blustered, as she picked up her reticule and pristine copy of Evelina. "Good day Violet, thank you for the tea."

Julia swept from the room with her head held high and her posture rigidly straight, as though good comportment might distract from her slip of the tongue.

Violet stood a moment, feeling slightly perplexed by Julia's uncharacteristic outburst, before turning her attention to the cups and saucers on the table. She began to gather them together to bring them to the kitchen, when Dorothy bustled into the room.

"Ach, my wee Violet," the Scotswoman scolded, "I can do that; you get back to your painting while the light is right."

"Oh, I'm finished for the day, Dorothy," Violet argued, as she continued to pile the cups and saucers upon the tray, "I shall take this to the kitchen then come help you tidy up."

The parlour room, like the library, was filled with stacks of books upon the floor. Though it appeared rather messy to the untrained eye, Aunt Phoebe had a meticulous system—if mysterious—and thusly, only Dorothy was permitted to clean the parlour room. Unfortunately, Dorothy had quite low standards when it came to cleaning, and Violet quite often offered to share the work.

Once she had deposited the crockery with the scullery maid, Violet returned to the parlour, to find Dorothy dusting whilst humming a maudlin tune.

"Faith, Dorothy," Violet said with a laugh, "It feels almost funereal in here with that tune."

"Ach," Dorothy placed her duster down, as she gazed toward the window, "Perhaps that is what this is. Poor Fifi is finally gone."

Violet glanced at the taxidermy terrier, who was still toppled on her side by Violet's easel.

"Fifi has been gone for over a decade, Dorothy," Violet offered, as she wondered if perhaps, the lady's maid and Aunt Phoebe had been brewing poitín again.

"I know that," Dorothy rolled her Skye-blue eyes, "Do you think me away with the fairies? I mean that her spirit has finally left us. Poor wee dog, perhaps she's gone ahead to sniff out a spot for myself and Lady Havisham in the great beyond. Perhaps death is nearer for us than I had seen."

Lud; Violet swallowed a curse. She had forgotten about Sebastian's fondness for moving Fifi to different parts of the house, in order to perpetuate Dorothy's belief that the dog's spirit still inhabited her body. Now, Dorothy had placed herself and Aunt Phoebe in the queue for St Peter, and it would be Violet who would have to suffer through visions of death and doom.

"And so from hour to hour, we ripe and ripe. And then, from hour to hour, we rot and rot. And thereby hangs a tale," Dorothy added, with a sigh so sad that the flowers in their vase near wilted and died from the sorrow of it.

La! Violet bit down on her lip to keep from growling in frustration. Instead, she picked up the broom and began to—carefully—sweep under the chaise, whose missing leg had been replaced by a stack of books.

Violet remained silent as she continued to clean, whilst Dorothy sang sad songs from the islands and made a half-hearted attempt at dusting.

Nearly a half-hour had passed, when Aunt Phoebe bustled in, wearing a turban with a plume of pheasant feathers, and her customary fox-fur stole.

"Dorothy," she called, "I wish to visit Ackermann's. I have it on good authority that they have featured me in one of their fashion plates, and I wish to ensure they have correctly captured my likeness."

Violet blinked in surprise at this statement; Aunt Phoebe's fashion sense was more abattoir than à la mode, and she was an unlikely candidate for one the Repository's fashion plates.

"A fashion plate, Aunt?" Violet queried, trying to keep the note of panic from her tone.

"Yes," Phoebe grinned, "Apparently I am modelling a coat made from a bear, and its head is the hood. It seems rather unpractical to me, but then what do I know of fashion?"

For a moment, Violet was not certain if her aunt was serious in her belief that she actually featured in a fashion plate, and not one of the repository's satirical prints, but then Phoebe offered Violet a wink, and she relaxed. Aunt Phoebe might be a curmudgeon at times, but she knew how to laugh at herself. Violet would not put it past Lady Havisham to buy said print and have it framed, for all her guests to admire.

"Perhaps we shall call in on Sebastian," Aunt Phoebe continued, directing her words to Dorothy, and not Violet, whose smile faltered at this suggestion. "I wish to upbraid him for not calling on me. Insolent boy; I could be dead in a week. Dorothy has foreseen a terrible accident, Violet, did I tell you?"

"Er, no," Violet replied to her aunt's mild remark on her imminent death, "You did not tell me. But there is no need to call on Sebastian. He called yesterday."

"I did not see him," Phoebe frowned.

"You were out," Violet lied, then sensing that her aunt needed more persuasion to stay away from Sebastian's empty rooms, she fibbed even further. "Though he did mention that he would be attending Lord and Lady Jacob's ball tomorrow evening. No need to go out of your way, when you will see him there."

"Very well," Phoebe sighed, "Anyway, he is probably still abed. He is like a bear with a sore head when woken too early for his liking—and then there might be a risk that I become confused and attempt to have him fashioned into a coat."

On that note, Phoebe took her leave, followed by Dorothy, who was all too happy to abandon her work.

As the door closed behind them, Violet threw herself down on the chaise with a sigh. Helping her brother chase his dream was a far more complicated task than she had first imagined, she thought, as she nervously wondered how the next evening would fare. She would have to spend the night pretending to Aunt Phoebe that Sebastian had just stepped out, all while trying to avoid the Duke of Orsino—though she did not feel truly committed to her second task. Unconsciously, Violet cradled the hand that the duke had held against her heart, as she pondered the coming ball.

Lord and Lady Jacob had invited half of London to their ball, Violet surmised the next evening. The grand ballroom, whose cathedral-height ceiling was supported by a dozen marble columns, was filled with the bodies of the ton. Beneath the three, glittering chandeliers, the great and good of the aristocracy mingled together, laughing, dancing, and drinking, and taking up lots of space.

Violet, who detested a crush, instantly felt herself freeze as she was confronted by the mass of people.

"La," Aunt Phoebe sighed, as she too took in the sight of the crowd, "How uncouth of Honoria to invite so many people. Has she no respect for my corns? I shan't find a seat out here, Violet; I shall repair to the card-room."

Violet, who had been bracing herself for a faux-search for Sebastian, held back a sigh of relief, though this relief was short-lived.

"Send Sebastian into me, once you find him," Phoebe instructed, before squaring her shoulders and disappearing into the crowd.

Although diminutive, Violet was able to follow her aunt's progress through the room thanks to the plume of feathers on her turban, which added nearly a foot to the five she could lay claim to. Once Aunt Phoebe had safely reached the card room, Violet began to scan the room for somewhere she might hide.

She sighted a shadowy corner, behind one of the marble columns, and had begun to push her way toward it, when a hand reached out and tapped her shoulder.

"Miss Havisham," a voice called, and Violet turned to find that it was Lady Olivia who had greeted her.

"How lovely to see you," the young woman said, and Violet had no choice but to offer similar sentiments.

Once that was done, an awkward pause fell, during which both girls eyed each other warily.

"Ah," Lady Olivia eventually began, rather awkwardly for one so assured, "Is your brother in attendance?"

"Yes," Violet nodded, wishing to escape, "I think he said that he was headed for the terrace, to smoke a cheroot."

"Wonderful," Lady Olivia beamed, her smile so bright and warm that Violet felt a stab of guilt for her deception, "Ah, must dash. Terribly nice to meet you again."

Lady Olivia departed immediately, no doubt headed in the direction of the terrace, where she might "bump" into Sebastian.

Violet, who hoped that the girl would not spend the entire evening on a fruitless search, continued on her path to the alcove. Once there, and when safely hidden in the shadows cast by the marble column, Violet leaned her back against the wall, and let out a sigh of despair.

She was not certain that she had the skills to keep up her deception for the whole night—not when it seemed that the whole world was keen to sight her missing twin. She was just pondering whether she might somehow fashion a Sebastian from straw—like the effigies of Guy Fawkes, which were burned on bonfires on Gunpowder Treason Day—when an interloper arrived at her hiding place.

"Violet," Charlotte smiled as she spotted her hiding in the shadows, "Fancy meeting you here."

"I thrive in the shade, not the light," Violet replied, in reference to their preference for playing the wallflower.

Charlotte grinned, before making enquiries after Aunt Phoebe, and finally

Sebastian.

"Pfft," Violet sighed irritably in response to her second question, "All I ever hear are questions as to Sebastian's whereabouts. I am not his keeper, I'll have you know. I don't note his every step. How should I know where he is?"

She had, Violet realised too late, spoken rudely to her friend. A cascade of guilt washed over her as she realised that she had taken her irritation with herself out on Charlotte, a perfectly innocent party.

"I do beg your forgiveness," Violet said, her gaze meeting Charlotte's, "I am afraid that Sebastian has been causing me quite the headache these days and I find that even the mention of his name sets me off like a cannon. Can you pardon my ugly outburst?"

The wonderful thing about Charlotte was that she was not one to take offence.

"There's nothing to pardon," Charlotte gave her a smile, "I know something of frustrating siblings."

Talk then turned to Penrith, and after some attempt at feigning indifference, Charlotte finally admitted to having fallen in love with the man.

As Charlotte despaired over her deception of Penrith, Violet thought on her own deception. At least Charlotte had presented herself as the right sex to her duke—her cause was hindered, but not lost completely.

"Most affairs begin under false pretences," Violet soothed, as she attempted to rally her friend's spirits "In fact, most social interactions are entirely false and contrived. Do men not seek to be seen as affable when they are first introduced? Do women not strive to give the appearance of a winsome coquette when presented with an eligible gentleman? I think you'll find that most everyone is wearing a mask, and the fact that you wish to remove yours and reveal your true self to Penrith before he is bound to you by duty and law is admirable."

Far more admirable, and far braver than Violet, who was trapped behind the mask she had made for herself, hoping not to be caught out in a lie.

"What type of trouble has Sebastian made for you?" Charlotte queried, seemingly suspicious of Violet's uncharacteristic loquaciousness.

"Oh, nothing untoward," Violet replied, pasting a smile onto her face, "I am lucky that he is not like most young-bloods, and that he is not making a fool of himself at the gaming tables. He is simply being Sebastian; nothing more, nothing less. Come, let us forget our troubles and go to save Julia—I have just spotted her in Lord Horace's greasy clutches."

Violet linked arms with Charlotte and escorted her through the crowds toward Julia, who was battling against yet another would-be suitor. As well as being legendary for his dull conversational skills, Lord Horace also infamously suffered from halitosis so bad that it almost warranted a formal invitation to events.

Once they reached her, Julia excused herself from her conversation with Lord Horace, and the trio departed for the refreshment table.

Charlotte and Julia chattered between themselves, but Violet soon lost track of their conversation when she spotted a familiar face, towering above the other guests.

Orsino, who stood a good head above the crowd, was wearing his customary scowl as he scanned the crowd. Violet was momentarily distracted by the beauty of his face in profile, and though she was supposed to be trying to hide from him, found that she could not help but stare.

She gave a little start as Orsino—perhaps sensing her eyes upon him—turned his head to catch her longing gaze. His green eyes widened, before he frowned with intent, and began to excuse himself from the group he was attached to.

Dash it, Violet thought, as panic and desire caused her stomach to flip-flop. Her attempts at remaining invisible to the duke had lacked somewhat in the enthusiasm department.

Oogling a man with one's mouth hanging open is hardly discreet, Violet chastised herself, as she pondered her next move.

Beside her, Charlotte and Julia had noted that another duke—Penrith—was making his approach. As Charlotte flustered, she ran a hand through her hair, catching the buttons of her glove in some of her curly tresses. Panic thusly ensued, and as Julia struggled in vain to free her friend from her predicament, Violet quietly absented herself.

Coward, she thought, as she slipped through the crowds, in search of somewhere to hide. There was nowhere suitable for her purpose in the ballroom, whose every nook and cranny was now filled with people, so Violet made for a set of double doors. These opened onto a darkened hallway, lined with portraits and suitably deserted of people.

As she traipsed down the hallway, Violet bit her lip, afraid of intruding into one of Lord and Lady Jacob's private parlours. But as she hesitated, the doors which she had just come through opened, and she realised that Orsino had followed her.

In a mild panic, Violet quickly rushed to the nearest doorway, opened it, and threw herself into the room. She closed the door quietly behind her, resting her head against the solid wood as she willed her heart to still.

In a moment, her panic had subsided, replaced now with an overwhelming feeling of shame. She was two and twenty years of age—a grown woman. Yet, here she was, playing hide and seek with a gentleman who did not deserve to be treated so shabbily.

"Gemini," Violet whispered aloud, as she steeled her resolve, "Be brave, Violet. Meet your fears face on."

Squaring her shoulders, in the hope that it might give her courage, Violet placed her hand on the handle and threw the door open, prepared to face her duke.

Unfortunately, her duke had been standing on the other side of the doorway, and as the door swung open, it met with a very solid mass.

Lud, Violet thought, as she emerged from her hiding place to find that she had not just faced her duke head-on, she seemed to have knocked him unconscious.

10 CHAPTER TEN

It was a point of pride for Jack Pennelegion that, in all his thirty years, no man had ever managed to knock him down. In Eton, he had never been the brightest student. At home, he had never been the favoured son. But, since his birth, Jack had been the sturdiest of men, well able to weather any blow.

Until today, that is.

The force with which the door had swung open had taken Jack somewhat by surprise, and though it had hit him, it was his own feet which had tripped him up and caused his fall.

Thus, when Miss Havisham's worried face appeared over him, like a vision of heaven, and she profusely apologised for her actions, Jack brusquely brushed her off.

"No need to apologise," he blustered, as he scrambled to his feet, in a vain attempt to regain some dignity, "You did not knock me down, 'twas my own two feet which did that."

Although it was something of a Pyrrhic victory to claim that it was his own actions which had landed him on the floor, Jack took some comfort from knowing that he was still the sturdiest of men. And he sensed that he might be required to grasp for whatever comforts he could, for now, more than ever, he was certain that Miss Havisham had won in her battle against her attraction toward him.

Why else would the chit have run when she spotted him making his way over to her?

Jack opened his mouth as he prepared to offer to escort Miss Havisham back to the ballroom, but she spoke before he had the chance.

"Oh, you're bleeding," she cried, with a startled glance to his forehead.

Jack touched a gloved hand to his brow, and it came away stained with blood. It was, he deduced, just a nick; he had certainly endured worse over his lifetime.

Miss Havisham, however, appeared to think him at death's door.

"We must staunch the bleeding," she said firmly, as she placed a hand on his arm and steered him toward the room she had just—so dramatically—exited.

"It is just a cut," Jack argued, unused to being the object of female fussing.

"A cut that is bleeding profusely," Violet countered, her voice firm, "You might not be hurt, but imagine the scandal if you were to re-emerge in the ballroom with a bloodied cravat. People might think you had engaged in a bout of fisticuffs."

"The ton does enjoy making babbling gossip of the air," Jack agreed, surprised to find that Violet had somehow managed to—gently—frogmarch him toward a chair, in what appeared to be one of Lady Jacob's private parlours.

"Do sit down," she ordered, in a voice which brokered no argument.

As a military man, Jack was as adept at following orders as he was at doling them out, and his posterior—almost of its own volition—hastily found a seat.

"You were right—it's just a graze," Miss Havisham observed, her eyes narrowed thoughtfully at the cut upon Jack's brow, "Though there's an awful lot of blood, for something so small."

Jack, with one eye closed against the aforementioned blood, which was dripping from his temple, watched as Miss Havisham reached into her reticule to retrieve a handkerchief.

"Hold still," she said cheerfully, as she stepped forward and placed her handkerchief against his brow.

"I can do that myself," Jack protested, rather feebly, for he was enjoying having Miss Havisham attend to his wound. And he was enjoying, even more, her close proximity.

Her scent surrounded him, floral and light and utterly delicious, leaving Jack feeling slightly light-headed. Though this dizziness could also be attributed to the blow to his head, he reminded himself sternly.

Jack was not accustomed to feeling vulnerable—or rather, allowing anyone else to witness his vulnerability. He was a man. A military man, no less. As such, he demonstrated a stiff upper lip and courage in times of adversity, never allowing anyone to guess at the turmoil that might rage inside him.

He had faced worse than a tiny graze on the fields of Waterloo and Friedland; he had bandaged his own wounds and the wounds of his comrades without blinking an eye.

But today, in a warm and well-appointed room in London, Jack found that, for once, he did not want to look after himself. He wanted Miss Havisham to tend to him. No, he needed her to.

"Poor lamb," Miss Havisham soothed, idly stroking away a strand of his hair with a soft touch. It seemed that she had acted unconsciously, for a fetching blush stained her cheeks as she realised the intimacy of her action.

Jack shivered a little, with a longing that was not base—not anywhere near it. He yearned, deep in his belly, for her to continue stroking his hair, to continue comforting him.

Very few people ever offered Jack comfort; it had, he guessed, something to do with his size. And his manner. The world viewed Jack as a rock, a sturdy man on whom they could lean for support. A man who would protect them at all costs.

And while Jack was happy to play this role, he realised—as Miss Havisham continued to tend to him, humming under her breath—that, for once, he wanted someone to support him. He also wanted to curl up in Miss Havisham's lap and purr like a kitten, but that might be taking things too far, he reasoned.

Dash reason.

"There we go," Miss Havisham said after a few minutes, gently removing the handkerchief from his brow, "It has stopped. We just needed to staunch the bleeding."

"My thanks," Jack replied, feeling the loss of her touch quite keenly. It must have shown on his face for Miss Havisham peered at him in concern.

"Are you certain you're alright?" she asked, her violet eyes holding his, "You did give yourself quite a knock."

No, I am not all right, Jack longed to reply. I want you for my wife. I want you to touch me lovingly every day, caress my cheek as I fall asleep. I want you to birth my children and allow me to provide for you, so you might care for them as lovingly as you care for me. I want to hear you hum in the morning, and gasp with pleasure in the darkness of the night. And when I die, I want the last thing that I feel on earth to be your touch. The last sound I hear to be your voice...

Of course, Jack had never been very adept at giving voice to his feelings. So instead of a romantic outpouring of love and longing, he simply delivered a curt, "Perfectly fine, thank you."

"Oh," Miss Havisham jumped a little at his brusque response, "All right."

Dash it; Jack cursed inwardly. He was making a mess of things. Why could he not be like Montague? Why could he not deliver flowery prose when it was required of him? Jack nearly groaned aloud with dismay, as he realised what his next thought was.

What would Montague do in this situation?

Thankful that his friend would never know his thoughts—for Jack would never hear the end of it—he paused to consider what the charming marquess might do next.

"Women appreciate being appreciated."

Montague had spouted this nugget of wisdom once and for some reason it was now all Jack could think of. Miss Havisham had tended to him, had ruined her handkerchief for him, and all he could say to convey the depth of what it had meant to him was a short "thank you"?

"Sincerely," Jack continued, his voice sounding more like a growl than anything else, "I cannot express how grateful I am for your help."

"It was nothing, your Grace."

It was Miss Havisham who now looked nervous, her porcelain skin staining pink at his words. She lowered her eyes, perhaps to escape the intensity of Jack's gaze, and he near howled with displeasure. He did not want her to detach from him. He wanted her closer.

"It was everything," he replied, reaching out his hand to take hers and pulling her gently toward him.

Miss Havisham's eyes opened wide, her breath slightly laboured, as she watched Jack turn her hand palm up and deliver a kiss to her wrist.

It was possibly the most romantic gesture that Jack had ever made in his life, but as he lifted his lips from Miss Havisham's arm, Jack realised that he wanted more.

He was not content to settle for a chaste kiss upon a satin glove. It was not enough; he wanted more. And from the desire which flared in Miss Havisham's eyes, he could see that she did too.

With a low growl, Jack tugged Violet down toward him, so that she had no choice but to fall into his lap. Her arms wrapped themselves around his neck, and this was all the encouragement that Jack needed to draw her into a kiss.

Cannon fire in Borodino. Gunshots across the fields of Leipzig. Neither of these things had startled Jack as much as kissing Violet Havisham. Joy exploded in his chest, desire coursed through his belly, and his very soul sang with pleasure as he claimed her lips as his own.

For a moment, he worried that perhaps he had acted in haste, that Miss Havisham did not wish to be ravished in a parlour room by a boor masquerading as a duke. But then she ran her fingers through his hair and whispered his name longingly, and Jack realised that she was enjoying the experience just as much as he.

Reciprocated desire was perhaps the most powerful aphrodisiac in the world. All of Jack's reason left his body, as he pulled Violet closer, savouring the feel of her warm body against his.

It was heaven. It was bliss. It was…dangerous.

Jack pulled away, breathless, as he realised that his desire was beginning to outweigh his conscience. He wanted Violet—but not like this. Not in a stranger's parlour room. And most certainly not when she was not legally his wife.

You could arrange for a special license, a wicked voice whispered in his ear, but Jack hushed it. Tempting as it was to continue with their passionate embrace, Jack knew that he could not live with himself if he forced Miss

Havisham's hand.

He wanted her to come to him freely.

"Wait," he gasped as he pulled away from her, "We must wait."

For a second, the only sound that filled the room was that of their ragged breathing. Violet, still perched on his lap, was watching him with eyes dark with desire, and something else.

Confusion.

It seemed that it was not only Jack who had been taken by surprise by the ferocity of their desire.

Violet's lips were plump and raw, and though they were always lovely, Jack decided that they looked best when they had been thoroughly kissed—by him, of course.

"I think," Jack said, his voice sounding rather pained, "That we had best return to the ballroom, Miss Havisham."

"Oh."

Jack instantly wished that he could take back his words, for Miss Havisham sprang to her feet, hastily rearranging her skirts. Her face was flushed, her countenance nervous, and she was—Jack realised—terribly embarrassed.

"It's not that I would not like to stay," he assured her, quickly standing up and catching her arm, "Believe me, I would like for nothing more than to continue this. But we must wait."

"Wait for what, your Grace?"

"Until we are wed," Jack said firmly, awed at the strength of his determination to make Miss Havisham his wife. Before, it had been but a wish, but now that he had tasted her lips, and had experienced the passion which lurked beneath her sweet facade, Jack knew that he would walk across hot-coals to have her as his bride.

"W-wed?" Violet stuttered, taking a nervous step back from him.

"Yes," Jack, recognising her fear, kept his tone even and calm, but did not detour from his intended destination, "Wed, Violet. I want you for my wife. Given what just happened, I think that you might also be amenable to the idea."

"You cannot wish to marry me," Violet protested, taking another step toward the door, "I am not suited to be a duchess, your Grace. I am not fashionable enough or poised enough for such a role."

Jack, who had been thinking the very same thing about himself since he had assumed his own title, shrugged his shoulders against her opposition.

"I am not looking for a duchess, Violet," he said, quickly crossing the distance she had made between them and taking her hand, "I am looking for a wife."

Jack held Violet's blue-eyed gaze, hoping to convey to her just how deeply he felt. Her lips parted, and Jack longed to kiss them again, but he held steady and allowed her to speak.

"I wish to paint," she protested feebly, "I have never wanted to marry. I want to see Venice and Florence, and learn from the masters…"

"I will gladly accompany you there," Jack rushed to respond, instantly warming to the idea of seeing Europe as a traveller, rather than a soldier. His imagination took flight, as he pictured them dining together on a sunny palazzo, ambling along the Tiber, and watching the sunset over Venice's canals. "I would never prevent you from pursuing your passion, Violet. If that is your only objection to my proposal, then—"

"—Your Grace," Violet interrupted, dashing Jack's growing hope, "Please. I cannot marry you."

Her voice cracked slightly on the word "cannot", and Jack wondered if perhaps Miss Havisham was harbouring a hidden reason for her refusal. Her hand was still in his, and he squeezed it reassuringly before he made one last attempt at persuading her.

"Nothing that you say could ever dissuade me from my belief that you are the woman for me," he said, hopeful that she would understand his sincerity.

"I don't know about that."

It was a whispered aside, but nevertheless, Jack heard it. He frowned, hoping to press her further, but Miss Havisham spoke before he had the chance.

"Thank you for…And apologies again for…" Violet waved a nervous hand in the direction of Jack's wound, as she stammered out her goodbye. "Good evening, your Grace."

On that note, Miss Havisham turned on the heel of her slipper and fled the room.

Jack remained where he was for a moment, staring at the closed door, his heart aching more than he had thought possible.

He had just proposed marriage to the woman he loved, and she had rebuffed him. Had he been misguided in his belief that Miss Havisham harboured similar feelings to him? Jack thought on their kiss and her passionate response and wondered if it had all meant nothing to her.

If so, that left him in something of a quandary, for Jack might now have to relinquish his title as the sturdiest man in England, as Miss Havisham had completely floored him.

11 CHAPTER ELEVEN

It had been more than a week since Violet had received her first—and most likely last—marriage proposal. In that time, Orsino had called twice, but Violet had instructed Henry to inform the handsome duke that she was "not at home".

It tore at her heartstrings to refuse to see Orsino, but it was, she reasoned, for the best. A quick, sharp cut was easier to endure than a slow, malingering wound. It would heal faster, she thought, though as the days passed by and her heart still ached, she morbidly wondered if perhaps her wound had turned gangrenous.

Amputation might solve my woes, Violet thought wryly, as she faced into yet another day of mooning over Orsino. Even her hands were consumed by memories of the duke, and when she sat down to sketch out ideas for her next painting, she instead found herself drawing the duke.

Soon, the drawing-room was littered with half-finished portraits of the man, though many had been crunched into balls in frustration. For, try as she might, Violet could not properly capture the beauty of her duke. She could not find a way to commit to paper the line of his jaw, nor the light in his eyes. It was completely and utterly vexing.

Thankfully, she had a meeting with her fellow wallflowers to look forward to, to distract her from her woes. As the clock struck eleven, Violet hastily cleaned away her sketch-pad and charcoals, as she prepared for her friends' arrival.

"La! Violet," Charlotte cried, with forced gaiety, as she entered, "What a wondrous day."

Outside, a rumble of thunder greeted Charlotte's words, and rain began to lash against the window, but the red-headed girl steadfastly ignored it. Her pretty face wore a determined smile, so resolutely fixed that it looked almost painful.

In the days after Orsino's proposal to Violet, Charlotte had been "greatly disappointed" by her own duke. Penrith had, it was revealed, only courted Charlotte so that his cousin might then be able to court Charlotte's sister, Bianca. Though at first, Charlotte had been visibly heartbroken by this revelation, in the intervening days she had adopted a very English, stiff-upper-lip, and had refused to discuss the matter any further.

Everything was perfectly, utterly, and completely fine, she had told her friends, umpteen times. Violet personally had doubts that anyone who needed to use so many emphatic adverbs was in any way fine, but Charlotte stubbornly refused to discuss the matter any further.

Julia arrived shortly after Charlotte, apologising—as always—for being late.

"Mama always has something urgent she needs to discuss when I am on my way to visit you both," Julia commented wryly, as she placed herself upon the chaise.

"Do you think, perhaps, she does not approve of us?" Violet wondered, with a wink.

The fussy Marchioness of Pembrook had made it clear from the start that she considered Violet and Charlotte a bad influence on their daughter. In her first season, Julia had been expected to find a husband, but instead, she had found friendship with the ton's two most determined spinsters, leaving her mother distraught. Though she was always the epitome of civility, when they chanced to meet, Violet was certain that Lady Cavendish would like dearly to bash Violet and Charlotte's heads together for ruining her hopes for her daughter.

"She would never openly say she disapproved of you both, though she did rather take a shine to Charlotte, when it looked as though she might become a duchess," Julia replied, rolling her eyes at her mama's capriciousness.

Charlotte's smile became even more fixed, as she sensed the conversation turning toward Penrith. Julia innocently levelled her friend an enquiring glance, before she gently broached the subject of the errant duke.

"Have you heard from him at all, Cat?" Julia queried.

Violet had to admire Julia's determination and bravery. Whilst Violet had quietly accepted Charlotte's wishes not to discuss Penrith—all while inwardly fretting for her friend—Julia refused to truckle to Charlotte's obstinate nature.

"He has written," Charlotte waved an airy hand, "Sent flowers. Et cetera, et cetera. He has apologised, and that's all there is to it."

"So, you forgive him?" Julia raised an eyebrow.

"I have accepted his apology," Charlotte frowned in reply, "It's not quite the same thing, but it's as far as I can bring myself."

"I think you still have feelings for him," Julia countered, her blue eyes knowing, "And that you are being stubborn, Miss Drew. Did you too not deceive Penrith?"

For a moment, Charlotte took on the appearance of a kettle about to boil. Her cheeks flamed red as her hair, and Violet was not certain, but she could have sworn that steam emerged from her friend's ears.

"That is beside the point," Charlotte eventually replied, through gritted teeth, before she re-affixed her face into a smile akin to that upon a mask of Thalia. "Now, tell me, ladies, what did you think of Castle Rackrent?"

If Charlotte had meant her abrupt change of subject to discombobulate her friends, it worked awfully well. Violet cast a worried glance at the unopened book upon the table, and Julia, similarly, wore an abashed look.

"Er," Violet twirled a strand of hair around her finger, "I meant to read it; honestly I did, but I—"

Violet cast a glance around the drawing-room, hoping to sight an excuse. Her eyes landed upon her easel, where her finished portrait of Aunt Phoebe and Fifi rested.

"I was finishing my painting," she said, adopting a pious tone as she continued, "One must work when inspiration strikes. It is the curse of the artist, Charlotte."

Charlotte's response was a sardonic lift of her eyebrow, but Julia leapt to Violet's aid by leaping from the chaise—which wobbled precariously—and rushing to inspect the portrait.

"Inspired," Julia decided, as she appraised the painting.

"Aunt Phoebe wishes it to hang in Havisham Hall," Violet replied, tickled with pride at the memory, "Alongside the portraits of other holders of the title."

Havisham Hall was the seat of the baronetcy, and its long gallery was filled with portraits of all the men who had once borne the title of Baron of Hebrides. As Aunt Phoebe had decided that it was Violet's portrait that she wished to hang there, it meant that somewhere in the wide world, one of her works would hang forevermore.

"Oh, how wonderful," Julia beamed, "And not only have you immortalised Lady Havisham but Fifi too. Where is the little monster?"

Violet frowned, as she glanced around the room. She could have sworn that she had left Fifi, glass-eyed and lying on her side, by her easel, but the taxidermy dog had now disappeared.

"Perhaps one of the maids cleared her away," she mused, for Hannah, the downstairs-maid, had been sneaking in of late to dust the spots which Dorothy missed—which were numerous.

Violet began to scour the room for the dog, poking through the potted ficus, and checking behind the ancient terrestrial globe, so old that it was missing two continents. Fifi, she finally decided, could not be found.

Whilst Charlotte too had joined the search for the missing dog, Julia had become distracted by something near Violet's easel. As she spotted what it was her friend was looking at, Violet gave a yelp, and Julia hastily closed the sketchbook she had been examining.

"I fear poor Fifi is lost," Charlotte called, as she wiggled out from underneath the chaise, her dress smeared with dust. "Perhaps Dorothy is correct, and her trapped spirit inspires her to wander the house."

Something prodded Violet at the mention of Phoebe's wandering spirit, but before she could examine it, Charlotte spoke again, distracting her completely.

"There is to be a boat race, on Wednesday in Hyde Park," she said, very matter-of-factly, "I feel it would behove us to attend."

"You do?" Violet raised an eyebrow at Charlotte's pious tone.

"Yes," she replied, her cheeks flushing pink, "Lord Horace and Lord Lucas have both bet an unseemly amount of money on whose toy-boat will be the first to reach the far side of Miller's Pond. I feel it would behove us to attend and demonstrate our disapproval for such a frivolous waste of money when London is filled with so much poverty and suffering."

Well. Violet was not so certain about staging a moral-protest at an event that was sure to be filled with the braying young-bloods of the ton, but it was nice to see Charlotte return to something of her zealous self.

"And afterwards, we might visit Gunter's," Charlotte added, as she sensed her friends' hesitation, "Bianca says that they have a new Gruyere flavour, which is to die for."

"I think I shall stick to my lavender," Violet replied, wrinkling her nose at the memory of the Parmesan ice she had once tried.

"But you will come?" Charlotte looked hopeful.

"Of course we will," Julia smiled, "I can't remember the last time we made an attempt at being paragons of virtue."

"The ballad singer at Speaker's Corner, last year," Violet remembered, before falling silent as she recalled how that particular endeavour had fared.

Charlotte had wished to object against a travelling folk-singer, who had taken up residence on the corner of Hyde Park, and was making a pretty penny with the performance of a very lusty folk-song. She had corralled Violet and Julia into staging an objection to his lewdness, which involved them standing with their backs turned to the offensive performance. Unfortunately, their protest had failed spectacularly and had actually resulted in a larger audience for the singer, as well as the composition of a new ballad, which while very catchy, also included some rather thinly veiled insults about Charlotte.

"Er, yes," Julia replied, closing her eyes against the memory, as Violet valiantly struggled against the urge to hum a few lines of "The Uppity Shrew of Mayfair". "That went...that went...Well, it went somewhere."

Charlotte, who had skin as thick as Aunt Phoebe, gave both her friends an encouraging smile—natural this time, and not forced.

"That's the spirit, ladies," she beamed, "It is not in the stars to hold our destiny but in ourselves. We can change the world if we but try."

On that happier note, Charlotte took her leave, promising that she would have a book selected for next week's meeting by the morrow.

As the door shut behind her, Violet cast Julia a mischievous smile.

"Gosh, she is somewhat back to her old self. I feel almost bad that I am only attending for the ice-cream aspect of the afternoon and not the world-changing part."

"I don't think even Charlotte stands a chance of saving Lords Horace and Lucas from their own stupidity," Julia grinned in response, "Though at least we will get to witness a little fun. Now, tell me, sweet Violet, what on earth is going on with you and the Duke of Orsino?"

Violet began to protest that there was nothing going on between her and the duke, but then she recalled that Julia had seen her sketchbook, and she flushed.

"I am nothing if not tenacious, Violet," Julia said, as she sat back down on the chaise, "And as well as tenacious, I am without any plans for the afternoon. Now, you will tell me what's going on."

"I would like to," Violet replied glumly, as she took a seat upon the Queen Anne, "Really, I would. It is just—"

"Has he compromised you?" Julia looked ready to do battle, "If he has, mark my words, I will run him through with a sword."

It was heartening for Violet to know that her friend would defend her against any egregious aristocrats, though Julia's outrage was more than a little misplaced. Orsino was not the villain in this tale, that role belonged to her.

"No, he hasn't," Violet said firmly, "But thank you for offering to murder him on my behalf. It would be no small task, given the size of him."

"Then what is it?" Julia pressed, not deviating from her purpose one bit, "You can tell me, Violet. I am your friend; nothing you can say will ever make that not so."

Violet hesitated, but the urge to share her burden was too great. In hushed tones, accompanied by numerous glances over her shoulder to the door, to ensure that it had not opened, Violet told her tale.

"...So you see," she completed, once she had adequately described her predicament, "I cannot possibly accept Orsino's marriage proposal."

Violet finished speaking and waited expectantly for Julia's reply.

And waited.

And waited.

After three minutes—according to the clock above the mantelpiece—Julia finally found her voice.

"Well," she exhaled, as she ran a nervous hand over her hair, "I really wasn't expecting that."

"You think me mad," Violet sighed, reaching for a French Fancy and morosely munching upon it.

"No, not mad," Julia argued, "Well, not that mad. Oh, if only Orsino had tried to steal a kiss, it would be far easier for us to deal with than this."

"You said that you would run him through with a sword if he had tried to compromise me," Violet countered, "I cannot see how a dead duke would be easier to manage than this."

"It might have some advantages in comparison," Julia was dry as the desert, "Though you're right. If we have to pick one scenario, we should choose the one with a live duke. Whatever will you do, Violet?"

Violet had nothing to say in response to her friend's query, for she had been hoping that Julia might supply the answer to that very question. If even the cool and unflappable Lady Julia could not remedy Violet's predicament, then perhaps all hope was lost.

"Just carry on, I suppose," Violet waved a hand miserably around the room, "Keep painting and hope that someday I might get to Venice."

And that someday I might forget Orsino, she added silently to herself.

"But don't you," Julia hesitated a little, before ploughing on, "Don't you want to fall in love? I can see it in your eyes that you love Orsino. If he loves you too, nothing else should matter. Nothing else at all. Perhaps if you tell him the truth—?"

"—He will have me sent to Bedlam?" Violet finished for her, though she frowned at Julia's newfound belief in the power of love. "Since when did you believe in love, Julia? I thought that you viewed marriage as merely a practical arrangement?"

"Look at the time," Julia cried, without glancing at the clock, "I'd best be away. Sit tight for the next while, Violet, and don't do anything rash. Well, anything more rash. We shall think of a way for you to fix things with Orsino, just you wait and see."

Violet blinked, in response to Julia's sudden decision to depart; she appeared to have ignited a fire within her friend.

"Is it Lord Pariseau who has changed your mind?" she queried, as she followed Julia toward the door. Something niggled at Violet's memory, and as she recalled what it was, she clicked her fingers—a most unladylike act.

"It's Lord Montague," she guessed, and all the answer that she needed was writ across Julia's face.

"I am late," Julia said primly, sidestepping both the question and Violet in her dash for the door, "Try to heed my advice, Vi. Don't do anything silly until we think of a plan."

Of course, as good advice as this was when a letter arrived from Orsino later that afternoon, addressed to Sebastian, Violet realised that while she might not wish to do anything silly, she did not have a choice in the matter.

The messenger has brought your father's reply, he wrote, I request but a moment of your time this evening, to ascertain what it is he knows, if anything. All going well, I shall be able to release you from your duties once done.

Violet willed herself to be strong, as she folded Orsino's missive in half. She would have one last outing as Sebastian, and then, she decided, she would commit herself to a life of regret for having tried to fool the duke who had captured her heart.

12 CHAPTER TWELVE

It was after ten o'clock when Jack knocked upon the front door of Havisham House. Dusk had given way to night, and the ladies of the house— Jack hoped—would be well on their way to whatever ball or event it was they were attending.

Had Jack called at nine, there might have been a chance of sighting Violet, but pride had—reluctantly, Jack had to admit—forbidden him from calling any earlier.

Miss Havisham had made clear that she did not wish to see him, and Jack knew that he must respect her wishes, no matter how much his heart protested.

As per protocol, it was Sebastian who answered the door to Jack's knock, dressed in the same clothes he always wore. Jack frowned a little as he noted this; thanks to Johnson, he had a whole room full of clothes, but then he was a duke, with endless funds at his disposal for such fripperies.

"Your Grace," Havisham croaked, in a voice that sounded as though he had recently been crying, "Do come in."

As Jack stepped inside to the darkened hallway, Havisham turned on the heel of his Hobby-boot, intent on leading Jack to the library. But on a whim, Jack bid him stop.

"The drawing-room shall suffice," Jack called, with a wave of his hand to the drawing-room door, "We shan't be long."

"Of course, your Grace," Sebastian nodded, though his brow creased into a frown, "Would your Grace like anything to drink?"

Jack shook his head to the question, for a drink would necessitate a trip to the library. Tonight, Jack could forgo his brandy, if it meant that he might sneak a peek into Violet's secret lair.

The drawing-room, much like the library, was filled with stacks of books.

Unlike the library, however, there were hints of Violet everywhere. A colourful shawl draped over the back of the chair, an unopened copy of Castle Rackrent upon the coffee table, and—Jack held his breath—an easel placed by the window.

"Might I?" Jack queried, waving a gloved hand at the easel.

He did not wait for Havisham's permission. Instead, he tread gingerly across the cluttered floor to inspect Violet's work.

It was, Jack realised as he took in the portrait of Lady Havisham, a very fine piece of art. The portrait depicted the irascible baroness asleep in her chair, with a taxidermy dog by her feet. It was a marvellous depiction of Lady Havisham, somehow conveying both her defiant spirit—after all, what peer would snooze through a portrait?—and her vulnerability, all at once.

"It's wonderful," Jack admitted, both awed and dismayed at Violet's talent. He had secretly hoped to find an asinine picture of kittens, so nondescript that his conscience might feel comfortable with trying to persuade Miss Havisham away from the dream of being an artist which was holding her back from him.

Instead, he had found talent; pure, raw, undeniable talent, which needed nurturing and feeding by the greats.

"It rather puts one to mind of—" Jack paused, as he racked his brains for the name of the artist whom Violet's work reminded him of, "Marguerite Gérard, that's who. Though your sister has not copied her style, she has interpreted it as her own. She is a very talented woman, Mr Havisham; look after her."

Sebastian made a sound almost akin to a whimper, as Jack finished speaking.

"I stubbed my toe," the lad explained, at Jack's questioning look.

"La! I do not blame you fidgeting when I am harping on like a fool," Jack grinned, "After all, I am here not to discuss art, but treason. Come; let us see what your father has to say."

Jack handed Havisham the message from Waldo and placed himself on the chaise longue to wait for him to translate it. The chair wobbled precariously under Jack's weight, and Havisham gave a yelp.

"Perhaps your Grace might prefer the Queen Anne," he said, waving to the overstuffed armchair opposite, "It is a little sturdier."

Jack duly obliged, noting that unlike the chaise, the Queen Anne had four legs, none of which were books.

Havisham strode over to the fireplace, to read the letter in the light cast by the dying fire. He hummed and hawed for a few minutes, before striding over to the window to fetch something to write upon.

"He has a name," Havisham called, "Just let me write it all out."

Jack stood, keen to see what message would be unveiled. He peered over Havisham's shoulder as he wrote, with a charcoal pencil, rather than a quill.

Traitor is in Whitehall, Waldo wrote, A Mr John Greer, though he has the name of someone even higher up the chain than he.

"Well," Jack whistled through, "Bravo Waldo. Your father has really come through for us. Might I?"

Jack reached for the page upon which Havisham had written the message, and as he lifted it, he caught sight of what was on the page beneath—a charcoal etching of him.

Jack blinked, a little surprised to find his likeness staring back at him, but then Havisham hastily closed the sketch-pad, and it was gone.

"Violet is always drawing portraits," he mumbled, clutching the pad to his chest.

"That's a portrait of me," Jack said, rather stupidly.

"No, it's not."

"It is," Jack bristled with indignation, "That is a likeness of me. I would like to see it, please."

"I am afraid that I cannot allow that," Havisham replied, sniffing with distaste at the very idea.

"I'm afraid that I'm going to have to insist," Jack growled, and he reached forward to snatch the sketch-pad from the boy.

The gentle tussle which ensued cast neither man in a favourable light, but Jack was triumphant in the end. He hastily opened the sketch-pad, before Havisham had a chance to snatch it back, and found not one, but dozens of etchings of him.

They were remarkably good, Jack thought, as he flicked through the pages. There he was frowning at something in the distance, here he was offering a shy smile, and in one, he was even sat astride a horse, looking magnificently regal.

Violet appeared to have memorised every line on his face, the curve of his brow, the point of his nose. It was most flattering, but also mildly perplexing.

"If your sister does not wish to marry me," Jack wondered aloud to Sebastian, "Then why on earth has she spent her days drawing pictures of me?"

"Perhaps she thinks you a good study," Havisham gave a sulky shrug, "You do have a very good nose. For drawing, that is."

"My nose is decidedly Roman and has been broken twice," Jack grunted, "At best one might say that I have the nose of a prize pugilist. Now tell me, why will your sister not marry me?"

"How should I know?" Havisham snapped in return, "Though your manners do leave something to be desired, your Grace."

"As do yours," Jack retorted, levelling Havisham's glare with one of his own, "I feel something is preventing your sister from accepting my proposal. A secret of some sort. But you tell her, you tell her for me, that I do not care about anything that she has done; I just want her for my wife."

Havisham gave a sigh that sounded almost wistful to Jack's ears. He glanced at the lad, who was standing starry-eyed, with his lips parted, as he gazed at Jack.

"I can also tell her myself," Jack decided, as he wondered if the lad had lately taken a knock to the head, "I shall call on her tomorrow. Dash. Not tomorrow, I have a vote in the House of Lords. Wednesday."

"I—I mean Violet, has plans on Wednesday," Havisham replied, clearing his throat and visibly shaking himself out of his trance, "The boat race at Miller's Pond."

"Then I shall call on her after," Jack determined, allowing himself a short moment to enjoy the jolt of anticipation in his stomach.

"Perhaps, your Grace," Sebastian said, his voice low and soft, "Perhaps you need not wait that long."

The lad hesitated before he took a step toward Jack, who was feeling rather confused as to what young Havisham was about. If Jack didn't know any better, he would swear that the young man was about to embrace him.

Rather mercifully, a loud noise from outside halted Havisham's progress across the room. It was, Jack realised, the sound of the front door being opened and shut. Both men were silent, as they listened to the intruder bumble their way across the hall, singing to himself in a deep baritone.

"Are you expecting a visitor?" Jack queried of Sebastian, who shook his head fearfully in response. All of Jack's primitive male responses rose to the surface, and he squared his shoulders as he prepared to face off with whatever villain was lurking in the hallway.

The intruder, however, was not content with merely invading the hallway of Havisham House, for a second later, the door to the drawing-room was thrown open, revealing a well-dressed young man, with a taxidermy dog tucked under his arm.

"Who on earth are you?" Jack queried, slightly bewildered to find himself confronted with a near-replica of Sebastian Havisham.

"Sebastian Havisham," the replica replied, further confounding Jack, who whirled to look at the real Sebastian, who was frozen in shock in his spot by the fireplace.

"And it is I who should be asking the questions," the replica continued, as he strode into the room. He glowered at Jack, before casting another glare at Sebastian, though this expression of distaste soon melted into bewilderment as he peered at him.

"Violet?" the replica asked, blinking in confusion, "Is that you?"

"Vi-vi-vi?"

For the life of him, Jack could not get his lips to form the name that had daily tormented him. He turned, very slowly, to face "Sebastian", and as he caught sight of the "lad", he almost laughed aloud at his own stupidity.

Violet's costume was impressive, there was no doubt about that; from the false-beard she wore, to the charcoal thickened eyebrows, it was all mightily convincing. But now Jack could see what he could not before; the diminutive frame that no amount of padding might hide, the thick, dark lashes which framed her eyes, and her hands. Jack gulped as he looked down at her hands; slender, elegant, and most definitely feminine.

He had been fooled, and worse, he now felt like one.

"So, all this time, you were..." Jack trailed off as he recalled everything that he had ever said to "Sebastian". He flushed, as he remembered having revealed to the lad that he had never coupled with a woman before. Lud, no wonder Miss Havisham had found it so easy to refuse his marriage proposal.

"I can explain," Violet said, rushing toward him, "I was about to explain before Sebastian arrived."

"Oh-ho," Jack exclaimed, as his wounded pride cast him in a pall of irritation, "I'm sure you were, Miss Havisham. Though I fail to see how there is any reason at all, which might necessitate you dressing as a man in order to hoodwink an emissary of the Crown."

"Lud, Violet. What have you been up to?"

Behind Jack, the real Sebastian Havisham gave an impressed whistle. Jack turned on his heel to glare at the lad, who quickly adopted a suitable chastised expression.

"I am sorry," Violet said, her face pale with anguish beneath her beard, "Please, believe me, you cannot know how sorry I am. It's just that your letter asking for Sebastian's assistance arrived the day after he had left for the north, and if my father were to find out that Sebastian had left—especially to pursue a career on the stage—there would have been hell to pay. I did not do this to hurt you, your Grace. I did it for the love of my brother."

Her words came out in a garbled rush, and Jack was not so blind that he did not see the anguish in her eyes. Missing brothers, a career in the theatre, a lady partaking in a real-life breeches role to save her brother from their father's ire—it was almost farcical.

Not almost, Jack corrected himself, it was farcical.

"I cannot fault you for wishing to protect your brother," Jack finally replied, when the silence became too unbearable to endure. "I too had a brother whom I would have done anything for—though I am not entirely sure that I would have stretched to donning ladies' clothing for his sake. I just wish, Miss Havisham, that you had confided your fears in me, instead of—"

Jack hesitated, as he tried to suppress the hurt which bubbled within his chest.

"Instead of trying to fool me," he finished flatly, hoping that his hurt tone did not further take away from the shred of dignity he had left.

Before Violet could reply, Jack leaned over to pocket the translated message, which had been cast aside on the table, and tucked it away in his breast pocket.

"Er," he said, as he straightened himself up, and adopted a serious expression, "It goes without saying that the contents of this letter are entirely confidential. I also trust that you will not share what has transpired in this room with anyone."

"Of course not," Violet breathed, her face ashen.

"Good. Insult to injury, and all that," Jack muttered, before hastily adding, "And state secrets, of course. Well. Goodbye, Miss Havisham."

Though a part of Jack wished to linger, and allow Miss Havisham apologise, pride forbid him. He was not oft guided by his ego, but in this instance, it had taken such a battering, that he could not ignore its yelps of pain.

Jack stalked silently passed Sebastian Havisham—the real Sebastian Havisham—who appeared to be valiantly trying to hold back an amused grin, and toward the door.

He half hoped that Violet might call out to him, or try to stop him before he left, but she did not. Perhaps she felt it too futile an act, given the circumstances.

And what circumstances they were, Jack marvelled, as he let himself out the front door onto Jermyn Street. The events of the past few weeks were worthy of a play, though should anyone care to write it, Jack was not certain he would have the stomach to sit through its whole performance.

Love, he thought mournfully, as he set forth for his carriage, was a thing suited to men far stronger than he.

The next morning, Jack set forth for Whitehall as soon as was possible. The translated message from Waldo Havisham was burning a hole in his breast pocket, and Jack longed to be rid of the thing, and be done with this stupid mission, at once.

Despite the early hour, Nevins was already ensconced in his dark, poky office, when Jack knocked on the door.

"Your Grace," the older gentleman stood up, rather nervously, as Jack strode in, "I wasn't expecting you. Is anything the matter?"

The man had lost some weight since their last meeting, Jack noted, and his manner was anxious. No doubt the business of capturing spies was getting to him.

"I have your name," Jack said, removing the folded page from his pocket and handing it to Nevins. "One of your own men, in this very building."

"Indeed?" Nevins drew his bushy brows together into a frown, as he scanned Violet's short translation. He tut-tutted a little, as he read the name of his traitor, but otherwise offered no other reaction.

"What shall you do?" Jack queried, slightly curious as to what the next steps would be.

"Ah," Nevins jumped a little, so lost in thought that he had momentarily forgotten Jack's presence, "There are strict protocols we must follow. Dull, internal investigations to be sure we have the right man before we send him off to swing on Tyburn's Tree—though, of course, not before we get the name of this higher up Waldo speaks of."

Jack shivered a little, as he realised that he had probably just handed over a man's death warrant to his executioner. Still, there was nothing worse than a man who had betrayed his country, and if this John Greer was indeed a traitor, then he deserved to hang for it.

"And you, your Grace?" Nevins queried, politely, "Have you plans for the rest of the season?"

Jack's current plans stretched no further than an afternoon brandy in White's, but now that he thought on it, a trip away from the city might be in order. He pictured the lush, rolling valleys of his estate in Glamorgan, and—even better—a strong pint of Bragawd, the local ale.

"I am away to my estates for a spell," Jack said, surprising himself, "Unless you have further need of me, that is?"

"Oh, heavens no," Nevins profusely exclaimed, "I cannot ask you to do any more than you have already done. My thanks, your Grace, for your help in this matter. You can trust that I shall remedy matters with Greer."

"Good luck on that front, Nevins."

With that, Jack took his leave, glad to be done with the sordid business of spies. As a soldier, he preferred face to face conflict, to the slithering and backstabbing of espionage.

The rest of the morning was spent attending to all the correspondence that Jack had neglected over the past few weeks. Jack worked steadily until the afternoon, stopping only for a quick luncheon of bread and cheese.

Once the hour struck three, he put away his quill and summoned the footman to arrange the delivery of his various letters.

"Does His Grace require anything else?" the courteous young Kimmage queried, before taking his leave.

"His Grace does not," Jack grinned, still slightly amused by the use of the third, "He will be attending his club this afternoon, so the kitchen staff may go back to twiddling their thumbs."

"I'll tell them that, your Grace," Kimmage gave a mischievous smile.

"No, you will not," Jack retorted, "For then I will have to spend the afternoon convincing Jean-Pierre not to leave. Away with you now, before you cause any mischief."

Dear Frederick had harboured a love of all things French and had installed a chef from the Aquitaine region in his kitchens. The man was highly excitable and easily insulted. Still, despite being as difficult to keep as a racehorse, Jack was reluctant to be rid of him, for he did know how to cook a steak to perfection—even if he was liable to fling it at Jack's head as a mode of serving.

White's was, as it usually was of an afternoon, filled to the gills with the aristocracy. The day's session in the House of Lords had ended, and the members of the house had duly filed into their members' club to discuss politics.

Jack side-stepped one or two gentlemen who looked as though they wished to chew his ear off, and nimbly deposited himself at the table by the Bow window, which had been left empty in expectation of the arrival of the Upstarts.

Next to file in, straight from the Houses of Parliament, was Montague, grousing about his new-found nemesis, Lord Pariseau.

"He spent twenty minutes pontificating on the plight of orphans when he probably eats them for breakfast," Montague grumbled, "In fact, I'm nearly certain I heard a rumour that he used them as live-bait to train his hounds."

"Really?" Jack replied dryly, "For I heard that he has pledged a considerable portion of his fortune toward building a new Foundling Hospital."

"Well, that's clearly just a cover," Montague blustered, before falling into a petulant sulk. "You're supposed to be on my side, Orsino."

"I am, and always will be," Jack replied evenly, "And as someone who has your best interests at heart, please listen to me when I say that you are being completely ridiculous."

"No man wants to listen to someone calling him ridiculous," Montague grinned, "Let alone pay heed to it. But you're right, I should not try to defame Pariseau—I should try to best him. How much did you hear he was pledging? I'm sure I could double it, triple it even! I'll show him what it means to care about orphans."

Orsino briefly closed his ears, as his friend began to outline the various ways in which he might help the poor, orphaned street-Arabs of London. When Montague got a bee in his bonnet about something, it was usually best to let him tire himself out. And, who knew, perhaps this time the dashing marquess might actually talk himself into doing some good?

Montague's ramblings were soon interrupted by the arrival of Penrith. Their friend had recently got himself into a spot of bother with his paramour, Miss Charlotte Drew, and his troubles had gifted him with a disposition as cheerful as a gravedigger during a plague.

Though, this was nothing as compared to Penrith's cousin, Augustus Dubarry, who shortly joined the men to share his own woes about Bianca, Miss Drew's sister.

Orsino listened patiently, as both men outlined the various ways in which they had tried to win back their sweetheart's hands, but one among the group was less than impressed with their efforts.

"You have written her a letter?" Montague hooted in amusement, as Dubarry finished detailing what he had done to try to win back Bianca. "No wonder the poor girl is ignoring you. You are not a clerk; you are her suitor."

The poor young man turned pink with indignation, as he hastily defended himself by arguing that he had also sent her flowers—though Montague was even less impressed by this than he was by the letter sending.

"What you need," Montague advised Dubarry, "Is a grand gesture."

The two men then began to discuss what sort of grand gesture Dubarry might carry out, but Jack did not pay them any attention, for his eyes were focused on Penrith.

His friend since their first day at Eton, many moons ago, Jack could tell—with just a glance—that the reserved duke was hanging on Montague's every word. Which meant, Jack grinned, that he must be in a bad way if he was going to take advice from the marquess.

As Montague regaled Dubarry with tales of his own grand gestures—which seemed to involve a lot of irritated abigails throwing buckets of water out windows on top of him—Jack debated how he might help Penrith. He knew that Miss Drew—who was refusing all of Penrith's calls—would be at Miller's Pond the next day, but he did not particularly wish to announce that to the room, lest anyone queried his source.

Thus, once their meeting had ended, and they were preparing to depart, Jack leaned over to quietly whisper this information to his friend.

"Miss Drew will be attending a boat-race at Miller's Pond in Hyde Park tomorrow afternoon, with Miss Havisham and Lady Julia," he imparted, "But for heaven's sake, please don't ask me why I know that."

Glad that he might somehow have aided his friend's romance, Jack followed Montague out the door of White's.

The marquess was waiting for him on the front steps, his handsome face rather smug. Evidently, he had enjoyed playing the role of a wise oracle of White's.

"You seem pleased," Orsino commented, as he fell into step beside his friend. Both men lived just around the corner, on St James' Square, and while at night-time it was prudent to travel by horse or carriage, a short stroll was commonplace of an afternoon.

"Who doesn't love love?" Montague questioned cheerfully, "And who could not be taken by the idea of Penrith finally finding it? And with a girl with spirit, not a laced-up Oizys, as I had feared."

"So, you knew that he was listening alongside Dubarry?" Jack queried, quite impressed at Montague's instincts.

"Pfft, of course, I did. I have known him as long as you!"

They strolled on in silence for a while more, rounding the corner of King's Street, where Christie's Auction House was located.

"And do you think Miss Drew will be amenable to Penrith's grand gesture?" Jack ventured, hoping to subtly glean a little advice from Eros beside him. "She was hurt, perhaps even humiliated by Penrith's deception. What hope is there for love, when one of the parties has suffered an injury?"

Montague was silent, as he contemplated Orsino's question. The sound of his cane tapping against the footpath as they walked was the only noise he made.

Jack rather regretted asking the question, afraid that his friend might realise he was really speaking for himself, but then Montague shrugged.

"Ruined love, when it is built anew, grows fairer than at first, more strong, far greater," he offered, his grin evidence that he was proud of having sourced a fitting quote from the stern of his brain.

"But what if Miss Drew is too hurt?" Jack pressed, not wishing to talk of building love anew when he was still smarting. "I mean, she must have been very upset. Humiliated even. No man likes to be made a fool of."

"Well, thankfully Miss Drew is a woman," Montague offered lightly, and Jack flushed as he realised that he had outed himself.

They had reached St James' Square, where Montague paused, as though he wished to speak further.

"I had best hurry," Jack said brusquely, "I am away to Glamorgan for a spell, to check in on the estate."

Montague raised his eyebrows in question at this abrupt announcement of his departure.

"It is imperative that I go," Jack blustered, as he felt a blush creep up his neck, "Ducal business. You will understand when you inherit."

It was a low blow, Jack had to admit, lording his title over his friend, though Montague seemed not to care.

"Ah, what a pity," he said with a sigh, "For I was hoping you might accompany me to a masquerade in a sennight. Never fear, perhaps I shall persuade Penrith."

"Can you not go alone?" Jack questioned.

"Well, I am not technically invited."

"Not technically?"

"Not at all," Montague beamed, "Though we must not dally over a silly ball, Orsino, when you are setting off on your travels to the back of beyond."

Jack frowned at this barb, though Montague did think that the world ended at the boundary lines of Westminster.

"I will offer you one more piece of advice though before you go," Montague continued, before adding with a wink, "Or rather, I shall offer Miss Drew another piece of advice."

"Go on," Jack rolled his eyes.

"He that is proud eats up himself: pride is his own glass, his own trumpet, his own chronicle," Montague said lightly. "Penrith did not intend to hurt Miss Drew, and I'm certain that once she realises this, and casts aside her pride, she will find that he has not left her heart. Well, safe trip, old friend."

Montague doffed the rim of his beaver hat at Jack and set off across the square, merrily swinging his cane. Jack remained where he had left him, for a moment, his mind ruminating over the marquess' none-too-subtle analogy.

It was true that Violet had not set out to hurt Jack; in fact, she had merely fooled him in order to try and save her brother from their father's ire.

But that did not take away from the hurt he felt, he thought stubbornly, as he turned toward home.

No, Jack decided, he would not cast aside his pride as Montague suggested; instead, he would go to Wales, where the mead was strong, and nobody was quoting ruddy Shakespeare.

13 CHAPTER THIRTEEN

"I say," Sebastian said, as he strolled into the drawing-room, "Have you ever heard of someone called Lady Olivia?"

Violet, who had been busy at her easel, poked her head out from behind it in panic.

"Ah," Sebastian grinned, "I take it from your look of terror that this has something to do with your recent escapades."

"Lud, it never ends," Violet groaned, as she downed her paintbrush, "Tell me, was it terribly awkward?"

"No, not at all," Sebastian wore the smile of a Cheshire Cat, "Rather the opposite, in fact. I have never had a lady walk up to me and kiss me, right off the bat."

"She kissed you?" Violet gawped, "What? Where?"

"On the lips," Sebastian hooted, perhaps thinking that Violet had meant something else, "We met on one of the secluded walks in Vauxhall, just last night. She called out "Sebastian?" and when I turned, she said "You are a most difficult man to find" and walked up and planted one right on my lips. I say, Violet, I must have you play me more often, perhaps the next time you pretend to be me, you might land me a fortune, as well as a wife."

"A wife?"

Violet pushed away her childish revulsion at hearing her brother's tale of being kissed to focus on the more pertinent matter at hand.

"Well, yes," Sebastian shrugged, "A woman like Olivia does not fall into one's lap by chance, only by divine intervention. And fate leads the willing, does it not?"

"I would hardly call my dressing as you a divine act," Violet rolled her eyes, "More a moment of lunacy. Are you certain you wish to marry her, Sebastian? You have only known her for an evening."

"But what an evening," Sebastian sighed happily, as he threw himself upon the chaise to gaze up at the ceiling, "Did you know that Olivia adores the theatre? We spent an hour last night, as we walked the gardens, discussing our favourite plays. Then this morning, when I paid a call at her home, we recited our favourite lines to each other over tea. It was marvellous."

"Nauseating, more like," Violet grinned, quickly ducking out of range of the cushion Sebastian flung her way.

"Don't play the cynic with me, sister dear," Sebastian argued, "I have seen the sketches for your latest painting. I know you are not as immune to love as you profess to be. Tell me, have you heard from Orsino?"

"He has left London for Wales," Violet sighed, "Henry tried to deliver a letter for me, but his footman told that His Grace had departed for his Welsh estate."

"We could go after him," Sebastian cried, sitting up with a gleam in his eye.

"Sit back down," Violet instructed sternly, "You forget that I am not a man."

"You're not always a man," Sebastian corrected, and Violet duly responded by flinging the cushion back at him.

Alas, Violet's aim was poor, and the cushion did not hit Sebastian, but the wall behind him, right beside the door which Dorothy had just walked through.

"Och!" she grumbled, "You donas, attacking an old woman only trying to do a day's work."

"I'm sorry, Dorothy," Violet offered contritely, "I was not aiming for you; I was aiming for this addle-pate."

"Well, you may practice harder if that's the case," Dorothy tutted, bending down to scoop up the cushion and lobbing it at Sebastian. Dorothy's aim was true, and the cushion neatly hit the back of Sebastian's head.

"You have to really want to hit your mark, lovey," Dorothy advised, as she began bustling around the room with her duster. "I learned that when I was in India with your dear aunt. Where do you think the tiger-rug in the library came from? It didnae come from a poor shot."

Dorothy winked at a rather bewildered Violet, who could not imagine the elderly Dorothy taking down an enormous tiger. But then, when she thought on it further, she actually rather could.

"Where is my dear aunt?" Sebastian queried, hopping up from the chaise, as Dorothy began to swat it down with her feather duster.

"She's in the orangery," Dorothy said, as she absent-mindedly began to dust Sebastian.

"Right-ho," Sebastian grinned, though his smile quickly vanished as he inhaled one of Dorothy's feathers up his nose.

"You must be coming down with a cold," Dorothy tutted, to Sebastian's loud sneeze, "Wait there one minute, and I'll brew you up a nostrum."

Dorothy abandoned her dusting to head for the kitchens, leaving Sebastian and Violet alone again.

"What is it that you need to discuss with Aunt Phoebe?" Violet queried.

"Well, I need her permission to marry Lady Olivia," Sebastian shrugged. "If Aunt Phoebe is amenable to the idea, she might increase my annuity, and when that is coupled from the wages from Whitehall, I will be able to support my wife in the manner she is accustomed to."

"What position in Whitehall?" Violet blinked; this was news. Well, further news.

"Orsino wrote a letter to the War Office, detailing my knowledge of French and the service I had already carried out for the Crown," Sebastian had the good grace to blush, "They called me in yesterday and offered me a position."

"But what of your dream, Sebastian?" Violet asked, feeling slightly tearful, "Don't you wish to follow your path and live the life of an actor?"

"Journeys end in lovers meeting, sister dear," Sebastian replied with a shrug, and his customary lopsided grin, "Playing Hamlet was a dream, but one that I knew must come to an end. How fortunate, that you found me Lady Olivia to cushion my fall back to earth. And not just a wife, but a position in Whitehall as well. Lud, I am deeply indebted to you, Violet. Would you like me to dress as you and see what comes of it?"

"Don't even think of that Sebastian, let alone say it," Violet objected, with a gale of laughter. She reached for the cushion on the Queen Anne and lobbed it neatly at her brother, where it bounced off his head.

"Gracious," Violet grinned, "Dorothy was right, you have to really want to hit your mark for it to work."

"All right, all right," Sebastian held up his hands in surrender, "I promise I shall not don one of your dresses. I rather think Olivia might object, at any rate. And besides, we have a plan for you, have we not? Venice, Florence, the great masters. Give me a year, Violet, and I shall have the fortunes to send you there. You can count on me."

"Oh, Sebastian," Violet smiled, crossing the room to offer her brother the warmest of hugs, "I know you will. Now, go! Go tell Aunt Phoebe that you wish to marry the woman you love."

Sebastian gave a flourishing bow in response and left the room with a very obvious spring in his step. As the door closed behind him, Violet gave a rather wistful sigh. How easy love was for some.

Violet picked up Dorothy's abandoned duster and began to tend to the room. Though she was happy for Sebastian, she could not help but feel slightly morbid about her own love life.

If only Orsino had allowed her to apologise more, she thought, as she flicked the duster across the mantelpiece, before she stopped herself. It was selfish to wish for the duke to have remained so that she might apologise and make herself feel better. He was hurt, and he had every right to be. Tempting as it was to force herself into his sphere, and demand that he forgive her, and love her again, it would not be right.

Violet had erred, and like anyone else who had made a mistake, she had to live with the consequences.

The rest of the morning was spent on cleaning the drawing-room. Violet assisted Dorothy with the dusting and sweeping, before tidying away her paints and easel in preparation for luncheon.

"Your brother has found himself a wife," Aunt Phoebe commented, when Violet arrived, newly washed and dressed at the table.

"Yes, he told me," Violet smiled, "It was sudden and unexpected, but then we wouldn't expect anything less from Sebastian."

"I don't suppose we would," Phoebe commented mildly, as she speared an asparagus, "And it is far preferential to traipsing off up north, to play a Moorish prince."

"He told you?" Violet gawped.

"I knew from the off," Aunt Phoebe grinned, "Nothing happens in this house without my knowing. Now tell me; what is happening with you and the duke?"

Violet, hurriedly tried to swallow the bite of fish-pie she had taken, before she choked on it in shock. She had oft thought Aunt Phoebe omnipotent—if scatterbrained—and now she had her proof.

"I fear that I upset him greatly, and injured his pride," Violet offered, after a pause, "There is no hope there, Aunt, but I am certain I will recover in time."

"Pfft. Men," Aunt Phoebe rolled her eyes, "They are oft so weak that a blow to their pride can be fatal. I had more hope for Orsino, but even I can be wrong. Well then, niece, if you do not think you shall marry the duke, then we must plan for your future."

"Is staying in bed 'till noon and eating copious amounts of French Fancies a satisfactory plan?" Violet mused, to which Phoebe tut-tutted.

"I won't tolerate idleness," Lady Havisham grumbled, sounding decidedly Scottish, "No. I think a jaunt to Florence, followed by Venice, then back round to Paris should be plan enough."

If Violet had been shocked earlier, she was dumbfounded now. How could Aunt Phoebe propose such a trip—which would take at least a year—when their finances were already stretched? And that was without the increased annuity to Sebastian.

"Thank you, Aunt Phoebe," Violet stuttered, "But it is too much. I should not like to be the Havisham who bankrupted the family coffers."

"You shan't be," Aunt Phoebe threw her head back and laughed, "Just because I like to live frugally, does not mean that we are impoverished. I have money aplenty, and a nest-egg that I have been saving for just such an occasion."

Aunt Phoebe heaved herself up from her seat and pottered over to the sideboard, where various miniatures and ornaments were displayed. She picked up a sculpted, wooden elephant, that Violet had seen every day for the past three years, and gave its head a sharp twist.

It opened to reveal a compartment, with a velvet bag inside. Aunt Phoebe scooped this out, tottered back to Violet, and offered her the bag.

It was heavier than it looked, Violet thought with a frown, as she opened its drawstrings to see what was inside.

"Aunt Phoebe," she gasped, glancing up at her aunt in astonishment, "Where on earth did you get this?"

"When I was in INN-JAA," Aunt Phoebe boomed, with a far-away look in her eye, "I met a rather nice fellow called Maharajah."

"Are you certain he wasn't the Maharajah, Aunt?" Violet interrupted, perplexed, but Aunt Phoebe was not listening.

"I had become separated from dear Cousin Cecil, who had accompanied me on my trip," Aunt Phoebe continued, "And I was frightfully worried, for Cecil kept trying to convert the locals, and they weren't too taken by that. Dorothy and I set out on a hunt along the Tapi River, hoping to find him in one of the villages. After a few days, this Maharajah fellow stumbled across us and offered some assistance. He sent several of his fellows off, to find poor Cecil, whilst Dorothy and I rested in his palace. After a week, Cecil was found, but by that time the Maharajah had fallen in love with me—not that I can blame him, I was quite the beauty in my day."

"Of course," Violet agreed; she had seen the paintings which depicted Aunt Phoebe in her youth, beautiful, wild, and untameable.

"Anyway," Aunt Phoebe shrugged, "He begged me to stay, but I could not. I had only just landed in Surat, and there was so much more to see! So as a parting gift, he gave me that."

Aunt Phoebe nodded happily at the ruby in Violet's hand. It was the size of a duck-egg, and a deep, almost flawless, red.

"John Rundell has offered me a fortune for it over the years," Aunt Phoebe grinned, "And now, I might finally take him up on his offer."

Violet was struck-dumb by Phoebe's tale, a fact which seemed to tickle her Aunt.

"Do you know," she continued, glancing fondly at the gem, "I tried to give it to your father when he finished up at Oxford. But he said he had heard enough of my tales of India, and seemed determined to set forth to make his own fortune, so I let him to it."

Aunt Phoebe gave a laugh that could best be described as a cackle and rose from her feet once more.

"I'll put it back in its hiding place for now," she said, taking the ruby back from Violet, "But it is there, and once we have decided on our plans, I shall sell it. Now, all this excitement has given me terrible indigestion, Violet; I must go take a nap."

With that, Phoebe returned the gem into its hiding place inside the elephant and took herself off to bed.

Violet, who still had some of her lunch left, remained at the table. She munched through her asparagus and fish pie, still quite taken-aback by Phoebe's revelation.

This is it, she thought, your life-long dream, handed to you on a plate. She should, she knew, be overwhelmed with happiness—and she was, not to mention gratitude to Aunt Phoebe—but still, she felt something was missing.

And that something was big, tall, and built like an ox, so it was no wonder she felt its absence so keenly.

After lunch, Violet took herself back to the drawing-room. She had no plans for the afternoon, and whilst she could have continued working on her newest painting, she felt too lethargic to bother.

Instead, she sat herself down on the chaise longue, to peruse the day's papers. They were still filled with articles about the marriage of the Duke of Penrith to Miss Charlotte Drew, which had taken place two days hence. Penrith's apology—and proposal—had been most romantic, and had involved a very public dip in Miller's Pond for His Grace, which Violet—not to mention half of London—had witnessed.

It was no wonder that the papers were still talking of it, though she did ponder, as she flicked through them if there were no other worthy news items they might report on.

Toward the back of The London Chronicle, there were several pages dedicated to notices—births, marriages, deaths, and the like. Other notices listed items for sale, or positions vacant, while others contained pleas for the return of lost cats or dogs.

Violet perused them with all the interest of one who was simply trying to pass the time, until, that is, a familiar name caught her eye.

Mrs Katherine Greer seeks information on the whereabouts of her husband John, who did not return home on Sunday last. The authorities have been most unhelpful. Small reward offered. Please write to K. Greer at—

Violet read and reread the notice, her mind a-whirr. Her father's message, which she had promptly forgotten about in all the duke-related-drama, had mentioned that Mr Greer held the name of a higher-up in Whitehall. Was it possible that this gentleman had discovered that Mr Greer had been labelled as a spy? Surely, if Mr Greer had been dealt with by the right channels, there would have been news of his capture—for the Crown did love to crow when they caught a spy. Something untoward must have happened...

No, Violet thought, as she tried to calm herself, that's ridiculous. Besides, Orsino would learn of Greer's disappearance, and investigate if he thought anything was amiss.

But the duke had departed for Wales, just two days later, a voice in her head reminded her. And it was unlikely that fate was so powerful that he would spot a small notice in one of the London papers.

Violet bit her lip as she pondered over what she should do. She could hardly march into Whitehall, asking to see the top-secret official who had worked with Orsino. Not only would she be in trouble, but Orsino would be as well.

Her eye caught on the front page of The Times, whose front page also featured an article on Charlotte's marriage to one of the infamous "Upstarts".

That was it! Violet said a silent prayer of thanks, as she realised that there was one person she could confide in —Penrith.

As Orsino's close friend—and another of Whitehall's emissaries—he was certain to know what steps needed to be taken, if any. And as Charlotte's friend, Penrith was unlikely to press her too hard for details on how she came to learn Greer's name.

Violet sprung from the chaise, in search of a shawl. She debated calling Henry to fetch the carriage, but as time was not on her side, she decided against it.

"I am going out for a walk," she cried as she raced through the entrance hall and out the front door.

Heaven only knew how many people spotted her, as she scandalously raced down Jermyn Street, toward St James' Square. But Violet did not care; she had to reach Penrith.

It was only at the front door of the duke's towering residence that Violet deigned to straighten herself up. She ran a hand over her hair, and wrapped her shawl tightly around herself, hoping that her appearance was neat enough to warrant admission.

"I need to speak to Her Grace," Violet gasped, as the officious butler opened the door, "And before you ask, I do not have a card. Please tell her it is Violet Havisham, and that it is an emergency."

The butler eyed her warily, but duly disappeared into the house—though not without closing the door behind him. After a few minutes, Charlotte appeared, having been dragged from the recesses of the vast mansion.

"Violet," she exclaimed, her face creased into a frown of worry, "Is everything all right?"

"Yes," Violet nodded, before correcting herself, "Well, no, actually. Well, if I'm honest, I'm not sure."

Charlotte took one look at her harried friend and placed an arm around her to guide her inside.

"We shall need some tea," she instructed the butler, "And French Fancies—actually, best make it a platter."

Once inside the elegantly appointed drawing-room, Violet began to tell her tale. She did not stop—not even when Charlotte tried to interject—until she had reached the very end.

"Well," Charlotte looked rather impressed, "I was not expecting that. What a tale, Violet; you shall have to elaborate more on certain aspects, once we have the time. But for now, I would think we had best involve Penrith."

Charlotte glided to the door of the drawing-room, no doubt, Violet guessed, on a cloud of newly-wedded bliss. She threw open the door, and poked her head outside, loudly calling for "Shuggy".

"He'll come quicker if he thinks the servants might hear me calling him that," Charlotte explained, with a wink, to her friend.

Indeed, in just a few seconds, the Duke of Penrith came striding into the room, his expression one of irritated affection.

"You hollered, wife dearest?" he questioned, with a sardonic raise of his brow.

"I did not holler," Charlotte grumbled, "I called for my dear husband, but you arrived instead."

"Perhaps your dear husband would arrive quicker, if you called him by his name," Penrith countered with a grin, before catching sight of Violet, "Oh, you have company."

"Oh, yes," Charlotte flushed, before making a hasty introduction.

"Violet has come by some information," Charlotte continued, once she had completed the necessary social niceties, "Though we cannot tell you how. I promise you she came by it legally—or well, I think legally?"

Charlotte cast Violet a questioning glance, and Violet felt herself flush as the Duke of Penrith turned his cool, blue-eyed gaze upon her.

"It was perfectly legal," Violet assured the duke, "I was helping the Duke of Orsino to translate a message from my father."

Violet was sure that Penrith wanted her to elaborate further, but she ploughed on before he had a chance to interrupt her. She quickly explained the message, and what it had said, before detailing the notice she had found in the paper.

"See," she said, thrusting the note, which she had ripped from the paper at Penrith, "Is it not strange? Surely the government would make a big show and dance about catching a traitor in their midst, rather than have him disappear."

Penrith took the notice and scanned it, his brow furrowed in thought.

Beside him, Charlotte smiled encouragingly at Violet, who offered her a wan smile in return.

"Did Orsino happen to mention who it was who was instructing him?" Penrith queried, after a pause.

He seemed, Violet thought with relief, to be taking her very seriously. She shook her head, and Penrith exhaled an epithet, for which he promptly apologised.

"I shall check across the square," he said, almost to himself, "To see what any of Orsino's staff might know, or if they might find some correspondence which might be useful. You two stay here, I shall return anon."

"I do love it when he acts so seriously," Charlotte whispered, her eyes following her husband's form as he left the room. Charlotte flushed a little, though her expression was one of a contented cat.

"Come," Charlotte gestured to the chairs, "While he is gone you may explain yourself more, Miss Havisham. Did you say that Orsino proposed to you?"

"Yes," Violet replied glumly, taking a seat, "Though I could not accept— not when I was deceiving him. I fear he might never forgive me, but do not fret, Charlotte, Aunt Phoebe has promised to take me to Venice."

"Oh, Violet," Charlotte gave her friend a sad smile, "How bittersweet."

"It is my own fault," Violet shrugged, "And though I am saddened now, I am sure that, with time, I will forget all about Orsino. And, it is better to have loved and lost than never loved at all. Isn't that what they say?"

"Mmmh," Charlotte replied absently, distracted by something outside the window.

The sound of the front door opening and closing brought Violet's attention to the matter at hand. Though, as the sound of two sets of footsteps approached, Charlotte turned to her friend with a grin.

"Perhaps all is not lost," she said, as the door to the drawing-room opened.

Violet looked up, to find not only Penrith but Orsino too, standing in the doorway.

"Violet," Orsino croaked, his handsome face wearing a look of longing.

Violet stood from her seat and stared stupidly back at him. Love, she thought, did rather tie one's tongue.

Charlotte clapped gleefully, as she glanced between Orsino and Violet. Though her glee was to be shortlived, for Penrith marched over and placed a hand on her arm.

"Come, let us give them some privacy," he whispered, though loud enough for Violet to hear, "Take it from a man who made a very public proposal—it is easier without an audience."

Charlotte looked as though she wished to protest, but she followed her husband from the room in silence. As the door closed behind them, however,

Violet heard a slight kerfuffle, as Charlotte put up some of a fight.

Evidently, she had thought that she might listen through the keyhole.

"Ah," Orsino said, as the noise died away, "Here we are."

"Yes," Violet offered in return, though she frowned as she thought of something, "Why are you here? I thought that you had left for Wales?"

"I realised when I was half-way there, that there was somewhere else I needed to be," Orsino replied, looking rather vulnerable for one so intimidating.

He took a hesitant step toward her, and when Violet did not back away, he took another, until at last, he was standing before her.

"I have been a blunderbuss, Violet," he said, as he took her hands in his, "A thundering, great gundiguts, and I should hang in chains for having run off like that."

"No, I am the gundiguts," Violet replied, though she was not too certain what that actually was, "I should never have tried to fool you."

"You did it for your brother," Orsino shrugged, before momentarily wincing, "And if I was annoyed, it was with myself, for being so taken in by your disguise. It was really very good; you could have a career as a spy if you wished it."

"I don't wish it," Violet held his gaze, willing him to understand what it was that she did wish for.

"Do you forgive me for being a prideful fool?" Orsino whispered as he lowered his head toward hers.

"Only if you forgive me for being a stupid fool," Violet breathed.

Forgiveness was granted between both parties with a kiss. Soft at first, but soon it turned to a more passionate embrace. Violet's arms snaked around Orsino's neck, as she drew him toward her, savouring his warmth and strength.

They carried on like this for a few minutes, both lost in the sensual pleasure of it until a noise outside the door stopped them.

"I wonder what that was?" Orsino looked alarmed.

"I bet you fivepence it's Charlotte," Violet guessed. And sure enough, Penrith's voice calling out an admonishment to his wife could be heard through the door.

"I'd best do this quickly then," Orsino said, as he dropped to his knee before her, "Violet Havisham, will you do me the great honour of becoming my wife?"

For a moment, Violet was so overcome with emotion that she could not answer. It was only when Orsino began to look a little panicked, that Violet finally found her voice.

"Yes," she cried, tugging him back to his feet, "Yes, of course, I will."

Another kiss thusly ensued, though this time Charlotte could not hold herself back, and came barrelling through the door, followed by Penrith.

"Oh, I am so happy!" she cried, at the same time as her husband said, "I did try to stop her, but she's unstoppable."

"Oh, hush, Shuggy," Charlotte admonished, and Penrith turned pink, "Anyway, we could not have left them alone another minute longer, or it might have been deemed a scandal. We can't fall at the first hurdle of our duties as chaperones."

Charlotte beamed, whilst Penrith turned a deeper shade of pink, as Orsino mouthed "Shuggy?" in question.

"Er, yes, quite," Penrith said brusquely, as he desperately tried to retain his customary formality in front of Violet. "Congratulations to you both. I wish you a long and bounteous marriage."

"Pfft," Charlotte rolled her eyes, "You are not the vicar, dear; you are their friend. If ever an occasion called for a hug, it is this. Oh, and some sparkling wine!"

Charlotte summoned a footman, who duly returned with four glass flutes and a bottle of sparkling wine. After a small toast from Penrith—which though formal, was endearingly sweet—and two glasses of the wine—which made Violet's head spin—Orsino declared that he would take Violet home.

"Perhaps I should chaperone you both on your journey," Charlotte cried, evidently wishing for the fun to continue.

"Perhaps you should not," Penrith suggested, treading not too subtly on his wife's toe.

"Oww," Charlotte yelped, before realisation dawned on her, "Oh, oh, yes you are right, dear. It's only around the corner, after all."

There was much hugging at the front door, as they awaited Orsino's carriage, and after a tearful farewell from Charlotte—whom Violet suspected had consumed far too much wine—they were off.

"Alone at last," Orsino sighed happily, as he followed Violet into the carriage compartment.

"We shall be parted again, shortly," Violet sighed.

"Not for long; I have every intention of calling on the Archbishop of Canterbury, once you are safely home, and procuring a special license. I cannot wait any longer than I have to, Violet, until you are my bride."

Violet made a few obligatory noises of protest, but they were just for show. In truth, she too could not wait until they were joined as one.

"But what has happened to John Greer?" Violet questioned, as the carriage took off with a jolt. In all the excitement, she had forgotten about why she had called at Penrith House in the first instance.

"Ah," Orsino grinned, "I must commend you on your skills of observation, my dear. Penrith showed me the notice. I will admit that it was naive of me, to take Nevins at face value—thank goodness you were here to catch him. Penrith is headed for Whitehall, after tea, to have Nevins' office searched. I don't doubt that he will swing from Tyburn's Tree by month's end."

Violet was silent as she thought on the fate of the faceless man she might have committed to death.

"His punishment is of his own making," Orsino said, as he took her hand, "Do not feel any guilt for that traitor."

Violet was silent for a few minutes, as she allowed the weight of the burden to lift from her. Soon, however, she realised that something else was amiss.

"Are we not home yet?" she asked, casting Orsino a questioning glance, "It is only around the corner."

"I'm afraid," the duke grinned, "That it is I who is now guilty of a small duplicity. I instructed the driver to circle the square for half an hour."

"Whatever for?" Violet asked agog.

"For this."

Orsino pulled her toward him, catching her lips with his, in a kiss that she hoped would never end.

"Do you mind?" he asked, his eyes soft.

"Heavens, no," Violet breathed, "In fact, I might ask the driver to make it an hour."

EPILOGUE

Violet had lost her husband, somewhere within the house. It was no mean feat to lose a man of six foot four, yet in every room Violet checked, her husband could not be found.

"Johnson," she queried, to her husband's valet, who was painstakingly attending to a pair of stained breeches, in Orsino's dressing room, "Have you seen His Grace?"

The valet shook his head, before giving a rueful glance down at the breeches he was attempting to save.

"Your Grace, I have not seen him since this morning," he said, before sighing long and weary, "But if my workload of late is anything to go by, I would assume His Grace is in the gardens, rolling around on the grass."

"I hardly think that is an act befitting of a duke," Violet protested with a laugh.

"Nor do I," Johnson huffed, "But grass stains never lie—nor do they wash-out. If you happen to find your husband, Your Grace, you might tell him that I am considering my position."

As Johnson threatened to leave every second day, Violet did not take him too seriously. She offered him what she hoped was a consoling smile before setting downstairs to continue her search.

The gardens of Orsino House, on St James' Square, were not so vast as the ones of the ducal estate in Glamorgan, but they were terribly pretty. A neat terrace opened on to an ornamental garden, behind which—cleverly disguised by a topiary hedge—lay the kitchen gardens.

Even from the doorway, Violet could hear the sound of her husband's laughter, and she set forth to discover what it was that he was at.

Violet tripped down the steps, past the trickling fountain, and along the stone-path to the gate which led to the kitchen garden. She opened it a crack and peered in, before bursting out laughing at what she found.

Her husband—all six foot four of him—was crawling along on his hands and knees, in an apparent attempt to teach their son to crawl.

Theodore, who had recently mastered the art of sitting up, seemed equally amused by his father's antics. Amused as he was, however, he also did not seem to be in any way inclined toward following suit. Her young son happily pulled himself along on his bottom after his father, gurgling happily at their game.

"No, Theo," Jack corrected with a groan, "Like this, on your hands and knees. Come on, lad, I have a fine Arab hot-blood wagered on you winning this race."

Race? Violet frowned.

"Have you entered our son into some sort of baby race?" she queried, as she pushed open the gate.

"Ah, Violet!" her husband hastily leapt to his feet, "My love, I thought you were off to meet with Charlotte and Julia."

"I was, but this letter arrived before I could leave," Violet replied, waving the letter in her hand, before she continued, "And I thought you were putting Teddy to bed?"

"I was," Jack shifted from one foot to the other, "But then, I decided…"

"To practice crawling for this race?" Violet raised an eyebrow, "Come, the cat is out of the bag. What's going on?"

"Well, the three of us," Jack began, looking rather shame-faced, "Spend an awful lot of time bragging about how brilliant our children are."

"Mmm," Violet, who daily bored anyone silly enough to ask with tales of Teddy's accomplishments, allowed him to continue.

"And it transpired that Penrith's little lad can cross the garden in less than a minute."

"He timed him?" Violet gawped.

"Well, it is rather impressive," Jack grinned, "Then Montague claimed that little Sarah, could do it in fifty-seconds."

Violet had a strong suspicion of the direction her husband was headed in.

"So," Jack dropped his green eyes, "I might have said that Teddy could do it in half a minute."

"But he cannot even crawl," Violet laughed, as she scooped her son up into her arms.

"He's quick enough on his bottom," Jack argued, as he stepped forward to gently stroke his son's head.

"Then why not enter him into the race that way?" Violet replied, so used to her husband and his friends that she did not even wonder at the absurdity of their conversation. "Did the other two stipulate that the babies must crawl? Teddy is very fast."

"I knew there was a reason why I married you," Jack grinned, as he planted a kiss on his wife's cheek.

"I am not entirely certain that is a compliment, my dear."

"It is," Jack enthused, now buoyed by their new plan, "I say, do you want to help me time him?"

"No," Violet transferred baby Teddy from her arms to her husband's, "I am already late for my meeting—and I am still not certain that I approve of all this."

After two years of marriage, Orsino knew well enough when to divert her attention, and so he nodded to the letter—now crumpled—in Violet's hand.

"What is it?" he asked, and Violet gave a start.

"Oh," she grinned, "It is from Aunt Phoebe! She and Dorothy have arrived safely in Paris. They will stay but a month, before heading onward to Florence. But, Jack, she showed my portrait of you to Marguerite Gérard, and she has asked me to come study under her for a few months."

Violet held her breath as she waited for her husband's reaction. While he had always professed to be supportive of her painting, she nervously wondered if this support would transcend from the abstract to reality.

"Why," Orsino exclaimed, as he gently placed Teddy down on the lawn, "This is wonderful, Violet. How talented you are—but, of course, we knew that already."

"You don't mind leaving England?" Violet whispered, barely able to believe her luck, "It might be for six months or so."

"I have staff aplenty who can manage the estates in my absence," Orsino grinned, "Do not worry about that. Nothing else in the world matters, my love, except that we three are together."

"Thank you," Violet whispered as she embraced her husband.

As often happened, this embrace became rather passionate—much more so than was proper for a garden overlooked by other houses.

"The neighbours might see," Violet laughed as she pulled away.

"Dash them," Jack growled, pulling her closer for another kiss.

After a few minutes, Violet somehow found the strength to pull away from her husband.

"Really," she insisted, "I must go—I cannot be late, for I haven't even read the book that we are supposed to discuss."

"You never read the book," Jack countered.

"That's true," Violet smiled, "But we have other things to discuss—chief amongst them, our husband's decision to race our baby's across St James' Square."

With a gentle kiss to her husband, and a smouldering glance to let him know that they would continue later, Violet took her leave.

How much fun she and her fellow wallflowers would have, Violet thought as she hurried across the garden, thinking up ways to put their upstart husbands back in their place.

A baby race, indeed.

ABOUT THE AUTHOR

Claudia Stone was born in South Africa but moved to Plymouth as a young girl. Having trained as an actress at RADA, she moved to New York to pursue her dream of acting on Broadway in 1988. She never did see her name in lights, but she did meet a wonderful Irishman called Conal who whisked her away to the wilds of Kerry, where she has lived ever since.
Claudia and Conal have three children, a dairy farm and a rescue lab called Bud.

Claudia is the author of thirteen Regency Romances, including the bestselling Fairfax Twins Series. Sciatica allowing, she hopes to be the author of many more!

You can follow Claudia on Facebook for updates on new releases and competitions.

Made in the USA
Monee, IL
07 September 2020